COLLECTION 7

Look out for other Goosebumps titles:

11 The Haunted Mask
12 Piano Lessons Can Be Murder
13 Be Careful What You Wish For
14 The Werewolf of Fever Swamp
15 You Can't Scare Me!
16 One Day at HorrorLand
17 Why I'm Afraid of Bees
18 Monster Blood II
19 Deep Trouble
20 Go Eat Worms
21 Return of the Mummy
22 The Scarecrow Walks at Midnight
23 Attack of the Mutant
24 My Hairiest Adventure
25 A Night in Terror Tower
26 The Cuckoo Clock of Doom
27 Monster Blood III
28 Ghost Beach
29 Phantom of the Auditorium
30 It Came From Beneath the Sink!
31 Night of the Living Dummy II
32 The Barking Ghost
33 The Horror at Camp Jellyjam
34 Revenge of the Garden Gnomes
35 A Shocker on Shock Street
36 The Haunted Mask II
37 The Headless Ghost
38 The Abominable Snowman of Pasadena
39 How I Got My Shrunken Head
40 Night of the Living Dummy III
41 Bad Hare Day
42 Egg Monsters From Mars
43 The Beast From the East

COLLECTION 7

Return of the Mummy
The Scarecrow Walks at Midnight
Attack of the Mutant

R.L. Stine

Scholastic Children's Books,
Commonwealth House, 1–19 New Oxford Street, London WC1A lNU, UK
a division of Scholastic Ltd
London ~ New York ~ Toronto ~ Sydney ~ Auckland

First published in this edition by Scholastic Ltd, 1997

Return of the Mummy
The Scarecrow Walks at Midnight
Attack of the Mutant
First published in the USA by Scholastic Inc., 1994
First published in the UK by Scholastic Ltd, 1995
Copyright © Parachute Press, Inc., 1994

GOOSEBUMPS is a trademark of Parachute Press, Inc.

ISBN 0 590 19445 3

Typeset by Contour Typesetters, Southall, London
Printed by Cox & Wyman Ltd, Reading, Berks

10 9 8 7 6 5 5 3 2 1

CONTENTS

1 Return of the Mummy   1

2 The Scarecrow Walks at Midnight   121

3 Attack of the Mutant   247

Goosebumps

Return of the Mummy

"Gabe, we will be landing soon," the stewardess told me, leaning over the seat. "Will someone be meeting you at the airport?"

"Yes. Probably an ancient Egyptian pharaoh," I told her. "Or maybe a disgusting, decaying mummy."

She narrowed her eyes at me. "No. Really," she insisted. "Who will be meeting you in Cairo?"

"My uncle Ben," I replied. "But he likes to play practical jokes. Sometimes he dresses in weird costumes and tries to scare me."

"You told me that your uncle was a famous scientist," the stewardess said.

"He is," I replied. "But he's also weird."

She laughed. I liked her a lot. She had pretty blonde hair. And I liked the way she always tilted her head to one side when she talked.

Her name was Nancy, and she had been very nice to me during the long flight to Egypt.

She knew it was my first time flying all by myself.

She kept checking on me and asking how I was doing. But she treated me like a grown-up. She didn't bring me one of those stupid join-the-dots books or a plastic wings badge that they always give to kids on planes. And she kept slipping me extra bags of peanuts, even though she wasn't supposed to.

"Why are you visiting your uncle?" Nancy asked. "Just for fun?"

I nodded. "I did it last summer, too," I told her. "It was really awesome! But this year, Uncle Ben has been digging in an unexplored pyramid. He's discovered an ancient, sacred tomb. And he invited me to be with him when he opens it up."

She laughed and tilted her head a little more. "You have a good imagination, Gabe," she said. Then she turned away to answer a man's question.

I *do* have a good imagination. But I wasn't making that up.

My uncle Ben Hassad is a famous archaeologist. He has been digging around in pyramids for lots of years. I've seen newspaper articles about him. And once he was in *National Geographic*.

Last summer, my entire family visited Cairo. My cousin Sari and I—she's Uncle Ben's daughter—had some amazing adventures down

4

in the chambers of the Great Pyramid.

Sari will be there this summer, too, I remembered, staring out of the plane window at the solid blue sky. I wondered if maybe she would give me a break this time.

I like Sari, but she's so competitive! She always has to be the first, the strongest, the smartest, the best. She's the only thirteen-year-old girl I know who can turn eating breakfast into a contest!

"Flight attendants, prepare for landing," the pilot announced over the loudspeaker.

I sat up to get a better view out of the window. As the plane lowered, I could see the city of Cairo beneath us. A slender blue ribbon curled along the city. That, I knew, was the Nile River.

The city stretched out from the river. Peering straight down, I could see tall, glass skyscrapers and low, domed temples. Where the city ended, the desert began. Yellow sand stretched to the horizon.

My stomach began to feel a little fluttery. The pyramids were somewhere out in that desert. And in a day or two, I would be climbing down into one of them, following my uncle into a tomb that hadn't been opened for thousands of years.

What would we find?

I pulled the little mummy hand from my shirt pocket and gazed down at it. It was so tiny—no bigger than a child's hand. I had bought it from a kid at a garage sale for two dollars. He said it was called a "Summoner." He said it could summon ancient evil spirits.

It looked like a mummy hand. The fingers were wrapped in stained gauze bandages, with a little black tar showing through.

I'd thought it was a fake, made of rubber or plastic. I mean, I never thought it was a real mummy hand.

But last summer, the hand had saved all of our lives. The kid who sold it to me was right. It really did bring a bunch of mummies to life! It was *amazing*!

Of course my parents and my friends back home didn't believe my incredible story. And they didn't believe that the Summoner really worked. They said it was just a joke mummy hand made in some souvenir factory. Probably made in Taiwan.

But I carry it with me wherever I go. It is my good luck charm. I'm not very superstitious. I mean, I walk under ladders all the time. And my lucky number is thirteen.

But I really do believe that the little mummy hand will protect me.

The strange thing about the mummy hand is that it is always warm. It doesn't feel like plastic. It feels warm, like a real human hand.

Back home in Michigan, I had a major panic attack when Mum and Dad were packing my suitcase for the flight. I couldn't find the mummy hand. And, of course, there was *no way* I would go to Egypt without it!

I was so relieved when I finally found it. It was tucked into the back pocket of a crumpled-up pair of jeans.

Now, as the plane nosed down for a landing, I reached for the hand in the pocket of my T-shirt. I pulled it out—and gasped.

The hand was cold. Cold as ice!

Why had the mummy hand suddenly turned cold?

Was it some kind of a message? A warning?

Was I heading into danger?

I didn't have time to think about it. The plane rolled into the gate, and the passengers were scrambling to pull down their hand luggage and push their way out of the plane.

I tucked the mummy hand into my jeans pocket, hoisted up my backpack, and headed to the front. I said goodbye to Nancy and thanked her for all the peanuts. Then I followed the others down the long, covered ramp and into the airport.

So many people!

And they all seemed to be in a hurry. They were practically stepping over each other. Men in dark business suits. Women in loose-flowing robes, their faces covered by veils. Teenage girls in jeans and T-shirts. A group of dark, serious-looking men in silky white suits that looked like pyjamas. A family with three little kids, all crying.

I had a sudden sinking feeling. How would I ever find Uncle Ben in this crowd?

My backpack began to feel very heavy. My eyes frantically searched back and forth. Strange voices surrounded me, all talking so loudly. No one was speaking English.

"Ow!" I cried out as I felt a sharp pain in my side.

I turned and realized that a woman had bumped me with her luggage cart.

Stay calm, Gabe, I instructed myself. Just stay calm.

Uncle Ben is here, looking for you. He'll find you. You just have to stay calm.

But what if my uncle forgot? I asked myself. What if he got mixed up about what day I was arriving? Or what if he got busy down in the pyramid and lost track of the time?

I can be a real worrier if I put my mind to it.

And right now I was worrying enough for three people!

If Uncle Ben isn't here, I'll go to a phone and call him, I decided.

For sure.

I could just hear myself saying, "Operator, can I speak to my uncle at the pyramids, please?"

I don't think that would work too well.

I didn't have a phone number for Uncle Ben. I wasn't sure he even *had* a phone out where he was staying. All I knew was that he had been living in a tent somewhere near the pyramid where he was digging.

Gazing frantically around the crowded arrival area, I was just about to give in to total panic—when a large man came walking up to me.

I couldn't see his face. He wore a long, white, hooded robe. It's called a burnoose. And his face was buried inside the hood.

"Taxi?" he asked in a high, shrill voice. "Taxi? American taxi?"

I burst out laughing. "Uncle Ben!" I cried happily.

"Taxi? American taxi? Taxi ride?" he insisted.

"Uncle Ben! I'm so glad to see you!" I exclaimed. I threw my arms around his waist and gave him a big hug. Then, laughing at his stupid disguise, I reached up and pulled back his hood.

The man under the hood had a bald, shaved head and a heavy black moustache. He glared at me furiously.

I had never seen him before in my life.

"Gabe! Gabe! Over here!"

I heard a voice calling my name. Glancing past the angry man, I saw Uncle Ben and Sari. They were waving to me from in front of the reservations counter.

The man's face turned bright red, and he shouted something at me in Arabic. I was glad I couldn't understand him. He kept muttering as he pulled up the hood of his burnoose.

"Sorry about that!" I cried. Then I dodged past him and hurried to greet Uncle Ben and my cousin.

Uncle Ben shook my hand and said, "Welcome to Cairo, Gabe." He was wearing a loose-fitting, white, short-sleeved sportshirt and baggy chinos.

Sari wore faded denim cut-offs and a bright green tank top. She was already laughing at me. A bad start. "Was that a friend of yours?" she teased.

11

"I—I made a mistake," I confessed. I glanced back. The man was still scowling at me.

"Did you really think that was Daddy?" Sari demanded.

I mumbled a reply. Sari and I were the same age. But I saw that she was still an inch taller than me. She had let her black hair grow. It fell down her back in a single plait.

Her big, dark eyes sparkled excitedly. She *loved* making fun of me.

I told them about my flight as we walked to the baggage area to get my suitcase. I told them how Nancy, the stewardess, kept slipping me bags of peanuts.

"I flew here last week," Sari told me. "The stewardess let *me* sit in First Class. Did you know you can have an ice-cream sundae in First Class?"

No, I didn't know that. I could see that Sari hadn't changed a bit.

She goes to a boarding school in Chicago since Uncle Ben has been spending all of his time in Egypt. Of course she gets straight As. And she's a champion skier and tennis player.

Sometimes I feel a little sorry for her. Her mum died when Sari was five. And Sari only gets to see her dad on holidays and during the summer.

But as we waited for my suitcase to come out on the conveyor belt, I wasn't feeling sorry for her at all. She was busy bragging about how this pyramid was twice as big as the one I'd been in last summer. And how she'd already been down in it several times, and how she'd take me on a tour—if I wasn't too afraid.

Finally, my bulging, blue suitcase appeared. I lugged it off the conveyor and dropped it at my feet. It weighed a ton!

I tried to lift it, but I could barely budge it.

Sari pushed me out of the way. "Let *me* get that," she insisted. She grabbed the handle, raised the suitcase off the floor, and started off with it.

"Hey—!" I called after her. What a show-off!

Uncle Ben grinned at me. "I think Sari has been working out," he said. He put a hand on my shoulder and led me towards the glass doors. "Let's get to the jeep."

We loaded the suitcase into the back of the jeep, then headed towards the city. "It's been swelteringly hot during the day," Uncle Ben told me, mopping his broad forehead with a handkerchief. "And then cool at night."

Traffic crawled on the narrow street. Horns honked constantly. Drivers kept their horns going whether they moved or stopped. The noise was deafening.

"We're not stopping in Cairo," Uncle Ben explained. "We're going straight to the pyramid at Al-Jizah. We're all living in tents out there so we can be close to our work."

"I hope you brought insect repellent," Sari complained. "The mosquitoes are as big as frogs!"

"Don't exaggerate," Uncle Ben scolded. "Gabe isn't afraid of a few mosquitoes—are you?"

"No way," I replied quietly.

"How about scorpions?" Sari demanded.

The traffic grew lighter as we left the city behind and headed into the desert. The yellow sand gleamed under the hot afternoon sun. Waves of heat rose up in front of us as the jeep bumped over the narrow, two-lane road.

Before long, a pyramid came into view. Behind the waves of heat off the desert floor, it looked like a wavering mirage. It didn't seem real.

As I stared out at it, my throat tightened with excitement. I had seen the pyramids last summer. But it was still a thrilling sight.

"I can't believe the pyramids are over four thousand years old!" I exclaimed.

"Yeah. That's even older than *me*!" Uncle Ben joked. His expression turned serious. "It fills me with pride every time I see them, Gabe," he admitted. "To think that our ancient ancestors were smart enough and skilled enough to build these marvels."

14

Uncle Ben was right. I suppose the pyramids have special meaning for me since my family is Egyptian. Both sets of my grandparents came from Egypt. They moved to the United States around 1930. My mum and dad were born in Michigan.

I think of myself as a typical American kid. But there's still something exciting about visiting the country where your ancestors came from.

As we drove nearer, the pyramid appeared to rise up in front of us. Its shadow formed a long, blue triangle over the yellow sand.

Cars and tour buses jammed a small parking lot. I could see a row of saddled camels tethered on one side of the lot. A crowd of tourists stretched across the sand, gazing up at the pyramid, snapping photographs, chatting noisily and pointing.

Uncle Ben turned the jeep on to a narrow side road, and we headed away from the crowd, towards the back of the pyramid. As we drove into the shade, the air suddenly felt cooler.

"I'd *kill* for an ice-cream cone!" Sari wailed. "I've never been so hot in my life!"

"Let's not talk about the heat," Uncle Ben replied, sweat dripping down his forehead into his bushy eyebrows. "Let's talk about how happy you are to see your father after so many months."

Sari groaned. "I'd be happier to see you if you were carrying an ice-cream cone."

Uncle Ben laughed.

A khaki-uniformed guard stepped in front of the jeep. Uncle Ben held up a blue ID card. The guard waved us past.

As we followed the road behind the pyramid, a row of low, white canvas tents came into view. "Welcome to the Pyramid Hilton!" Uncle Ben joked. "That's our luxury suite over there." He pointed to the nearest tent.

"It's pretty comfortable," he said, parking the jeep beside the tent. "But the room service is lousy."

"And you have to watch out for scorpions," Sari warned.

She'd say *anything* to try to scare me.

We unloaded my suitcase. Then Uncle Ben led us up to the base of the pyramid.

A camera crew was packing up its equipment. A young man, covered in dust, climbed out of a low entrance dug into one of the limestone squares. He waved to my uncle, then hurried towards the tents.

"One of my people," Uncle Ben muttered. He motioned towards the pyramid. "Well, here you are, Gabe. A long way from Michigan, huh?"

I nodded. "It's amazing," I told him, shielding my eyes to gaze up to the top. "I'd forgotten how much bigger the pyramids look in person."

"Tomorrow I'll take you both down to the tomb," Uncle Ben promised. "You've come at just the right time. We've been digging for months and months. And at long last, we are about to break the seal and enter the tomb itself."

"Wow!" I exclaimed. I wanted to be cool in front of Sari. But I couldn't help it. I was really excited.

"Guess you'll be really famous after you open the tomb, huh, Dad?" Sari asked. She swatted a fly on her arm. "Ow!"

"I'll be so famous, the flies will be afraid to bite you," Uncle Ben replied. "By the way, do you know what they called flies in ancient Egypt?"

Sari and I shook our heads no.

"I don't either!" Uncle Ben said, grinning. One of his stupid jokes. He had an endless supply of them. His expression suddenly changed. "Oh. That reminds me. I have a present for you, Gabe."

"A present?"

"Now, where did I put it?" He dug both hands into the pockets of his baggy chinos.

As he searched, I saw something move behind him. A shadow over my uncle's shoulder, back at the low opening to the pyramid.

I squinted at it.

The shadow moved. A figure stepped out slowly.

17

At first I thought the sun was playing tricks on my eyes.

But as I squinted harder, I realized that I was seeing correctly.

The figure stepped out from the pyramid—its face was covered in worn, yellowed gauze. So were its arms. And its legs.

I opened my mouth to cry out—but my voice choked in my throat.

And as I struggled to alert my uncle, the mummy stiffly stretched out its arms and came staggering up behind him.

I saw Sari's eyes grow wide with fright. She let out a low gasp.

"Uncle Ben—!" I finally managed to scream. "Turn around! It—it—!"

My uncle narrowed his eyes at me, confused.

The mummy staggered closer, its hands reaching out menacingly, about to grab the back of Uncle Ben's neck.

"A *mummy!*" I shrieked.

Uncle Ben spun around. He let out a startled cry. "It walks!" he shouted, pointing at the mummy with a trembling finger. He backed away as the mummy advanced. "It walks!"

"Ohhh." A strange moan escaped Sari's lips.

I turned and started to run.

But then the mummy burst out laughing.

It lowered its yellowed arms. "Boo!" it cried, and laughed again.

I turned and saw that Uncle Ben was laughing, too. His dark eyes sparkled gleefully. "It

19

walks! It walks!" he repeated, shaking his head. He put his arm around the mummy's shoulder.

I gaped at the two of them, my heart still pounding.

"This is John," Uncle Ben said, enjoying the joke he'd pulled on us. "He's been doing a TV advert here. For some new kind of stickier bandage."

"Sticky Bird Bandages," John told us. "They're just what your mummy ordered!"

He and Uncle Ben enjoyed another good laugh at that. Then my uncle pointed to the camera crew, packing their equipment into a small van. "They've finished for the day. But John agreed to hang around and help me scare you."

Sari rolled her eyes. "Nice try," she said dryly. "You'll have to do better than that, Daddy, to frighten me." And then she added, "Poor Gabe. Did you see his face? He was so freaked out! I thought he was going to spontaneously *combust* or something!"

Uncle Ben and John laughed.

"Hey—no way!" I insisted, feeling my face turn red.

How could Sari *say* that? When the mummy staggered out, I saw her gasp and back away. She was just as scared as I was!

"I heard you scream, too!" I told her. I didn't mean to sound so whiny.

"I just did that to help them scare you," Sari

insisted. She tossed her long plait over her shoulder.

"I've got to run," John said, glancing at his wristwatch. "As soon as we get back to the hotel, I'm going to hit the pool. I may stay underwater for a week!" He gave us a wave of his bandaged hand and went jogging to the van.

Why hadn't I noticed that he was wearing a wristwatch?

I felt like a total dork. "That's it!" I cried angrily to my uncle. "I'm never falling for one of your stupid jokes again! Never!"

He grinned at me and winked. "Want to bet?"

"What about Gabe's present?" Sari asked. "What is it?"

Uncle Ben pulled something out of his pocket and held it up. A pendant on a string. Made of clear orange glass. It gleamed in the bright sunlight.

He handed it to me. I moved it in my hand, feeling its smoothness as I examined it. "What is it?" I asked him. "What kind of glass is this?"

"It isn't glass," he replied. "It's a clear stone called amber." He stepped closer to examine it along with me. "Hold it up and look inside the pendant."

I followed his instructions. I saw a large brown bug inside. "It looks like some kind of beetle," I said.

"It *is* a beetle," Uncle Ben said, squinting one

21

eye to see it better. "It's an ancient beetle called a *scarab*. It was trapped in the amber four thousand years ago. As you can see, it's perfectly preserved."

"That's really gross," Sari commented, making a face. She slapped Uncle Ben on the back. "Great gift, Dad. A dead bug. Remind me not to let you do our Christmas shopping!"

Uncle Ben laughed. Then he turned back to me. "The scarab was very important to the ancient Egyptians," he said, rolling the amber pendant in his fingers, then dropping it back into my palm. "They believed that scarabs were a symbol of immortality."

I stared at the bug's dark shell, its six prickly legs, perfectly preserved.

"To keep a scarab meant immortality," my uncle continued. "But the bite of a scarab meant instant death."

"Weird," Sari muttered.

"It's great-looking," I told him. "Is it really four thousand years old?"

He nodded. "Wear it around your neck, Gabe. Maybe it still has some of its ancient powers."

I slipped the pendant over my head and adjusted it under my T-shirt. The amber stone felt cool against my skin. "Thanks, Uncle Ben," I said. "It's a great present."

He mopped his sweaty forehead with a wadded-up handkerchief. "Let's go back to the tent and get something cold to drink," he said.

We took a few steps—and then stopped when we saw Sari's face.

Her entire body trembled. Her mouth dropped open as she pointed to my chest.

"Sari—what *is* it?" Uncle Ben cried.

"The s-scarab—" she stammered. "It . . . escaped! I saw it!" She pointed down. "It's there!"

"Huh?" I spun away from her and bent down to find the scarab.

"Ow!" I cried out when I felt a sharp stab of pain on the back of my leg.

And realized the scarab had bitten me.

As I gasped in alarm, Uncle Ben's words about the scarab rushed through my mind.

"To keep a scarab meant immortality. But the bite of a scarab meant instant death."

Instant death?

"Noooo!" I let out a howl and spun around.

And saw Sari hunched down on her knees. Grinning. Her hand outstretched.

And realized she had pinched my leg.

My heart still pounding, I grabbed the pendant and stared into the orange glassy stone. The scarab was still frozen inside, just as it had been for four thousand years.

"Aaaaaaaggh!" I let out a howl of rage. I was mostly furious at myself.

Was I going to fall for every stupid joke Uncle Ben and Sari played on me this trip? If so, it was going to be a very long summer.

I had always liked my cousin. Except for the times when she was being so competitive and so superior, we always got along really well.

But now I wanted to punch her. I wanted to say really nasty things to her.

But I couldn't think of anything nasty enough.

"That was really mean, Sari," I said glumly, tucking the pendant under my T-shirt.

"Yes, it was—*wasn't* it!" she replied, very pleased with herself.

That night, I lay on my back on my narrow camp bed, staring up at the low tent roof, listening. Listening to the brush of the wind against the tent door, the soft creak of the tent poles, the flap of the canvas.

I don't think I'd ever felt so alert.

Turning my head, I could see the pale glow of moonlight through a crack in the tent door. I could see blades of dried desert grass on the sand outside. I could see water stains on the tent wall over my bed.

I'll never get to sleep, I thought unhappily.

I pushed and punched the flat pillow for the twentieth time, trying to fluff it up. The harsh wool blanket felt scratchy against my chin.

I'd slept away from home before. But I'd always slept in a room of some kind. Not in the middle of a vast, sandy desert in a tiny, flapping, creaking, canvas tent.

I wasn't scared. My uncle lay snoring away in his bed a few feet across the tent.

I was just alert. Very, very alert.

So alert I could hear the swish of palm trees outside. And I could hear the low hum of car tyres miles away on the narrow road.

And I heard the thudding of my heart when something wriggled on my chest.

I was so alert. I felt it instantly.

Just a tickle. A quick, light move.

It could only be one thing. The scarab moving inside the amber pendant.

No joke this time.

No joke. It moved.

I fumbled for the pendant in the dark, tossing down the blanket. I held it up to the moonlight. I could see the fat beetle in there, black in its orange prison.

"Did you move?" I whispered to it. "Did you wriggle your legs?"

I suddenly felt really stupid. Why was I whispering to a four-thousand-year-old insect? Why was I imagining that it was alive?

Annoyed with myself, I tucked the pendant back under my nightshirt.

I had no way of knowing how important that pendant would soon become to me.

I had no way of knowing that the pendant held a secret that would either save my life. Or kill me.

The tent was already hot when I awoke the next morning. Bright yellow sunlight poured in through the open tent flap. Squinting against the light, I rubbed my eyes and stretched. Uncle Ben had already gone out.

My back ached. The camp bed was so hard!

But I was too excited to worry about my back. I was going down into the pyramid this morning to the entrance of an ancient tomb.

I pulled on a clean T-shirt and the jeans I'd worn the day before. I adjusted the scarab pendant under the T-shirt. Then I carefully tucked the little mummy hand into the back pocket of my jeans.

With the pendant and the mummy hand, I'm well protected, I told myself. Nothing bad can happen on this trip.

I pulled a hairbrush through my thick, black hair a few times, and tugged my black-and-yellow Michigan Wolverines cap on. Then I hurried to the mess tent to get some breakfast.

The sun was floating above the palm trees in the distance. The yellow desert sand gleamed brightly. I took a deep breath of fresh air.

Yuck. There must be some camels nearby, I decided. The air wasn't exactly fresh.

I found Sari and Uncle Ben having their breakfast, seated at the end of the long table in the mess tent. Uncle Ben wore his usual baggy chinos and a short-sleeved, white sportshirt with coffee stains down the front.

Sari had her long, black hair pulled straight back in a ponytail. She wore a bright red tank top over white tennis shorts.

They greeted me as I entered the tent. I poured myself a glass of orange juice and, since I didn't see any Frosted Flakes, filled a bowl with raisin bran.

Three of Uncle Ben's workers were eating at the other end of the table. They were talking excitedly about their work. "We could go in today," I heard one of them say.

"It might take days to break the seal on the tomb door," a young woman replied.

I sat down next to Sari. "Tell me all about the tomb," I said to Uncle Ben. "Whose tomb is it? What's in there?"

He chuckled. "Let me say good morning before I launch into a lecture."

Sari leaned over my cereal bowl. "Hey, look—" she said, pointing. "I got a lot more raisins than you did!"

I *told* you she could turn breakfast into a contest.

"Well, I got more pulp in my orange juice," I replied.

It was just a joke, but she checked her juice glass to make sure.

Uncle Ben wiped his mouth with a paper napkin. He took a long sip of black coffee. "If I'm not mistaken," he began, "the tomb we have discovered here belonged to a prince. Actually, a cousin of King Tutankhamen."

"That's King Tut," Sari told me, interrupting.

"I know that!" I replied sharply.

"King Tut's tomb was discovered in 1922," Uncle Ben continued. "The vast burial chamber was filled with most of Tut's treasures. It was the most amazing archaeological discovery of the century." A smile crossed his face. "Until now."

"Do you think you've found something even more amazing?" I asked. I hadn't touched my cereal. I was too interested in my uncle's story.

He shrugged. "There's no way of knowing what's behind the tomb door until we open it, Gabe. But I have my fingers crossed. I believe we've found the burial chamber of Prince

Khor-Ru. He was the king's cousin. And he was said to be as wealthy as the king."

"And do you think all of Prince Khor-Ru's crowns, and jewels and belongings are buried with him?" Sari asked.

Uncle Ben took the last sip of coffee and slid the white mug across the table. "Who knows?" he replied. "There could be amazing treasures in there. Or it could be empty. Just an empty room."

"How could it be empty?" I demanded. "Why would there be an empty tomb in the pyramids?"

"Grave robbers," Uncle Ben replied, frowning. "Remember, Prince Khor-Ru was buried sometime around 1300 BC. Over the centuries, thieves broke into the pyramids and robbed the treasures from many burial chambers."

He stood up and sighed. "We may have been digging for all these months only to find an empty room."

"No way!" I cried excitedly. "I bet we will find the Prince's mummy in there. And millions of pounds' worth of jewels!"

Uncle Ben smiled at me. "Enough talk," he said. "Finish your breakfast so we can go and find out."

Sari and I followed Uncle Ben out of the tent. He waved to two young men who came out of the supply tent carrying digging equipment. Then he hurried over to talk to them.

Sari and I lingered back. She turned to me, a serious expression on her face. "Hey, Gabe," she said softly, "sorry I've been such a pain."

"You? A pain?" I replied sarcastically.

She didn't laugh. "I'm a bit worried," she confessed. "About Daddy."

I glanced at Uncle Ben. He was slapping one of the young men on the back as he talked. His usual jolly self.

"Why are you worried?" I asked Sari. "Your dad is in a great mood."

"That's why I'm worried," Sari whispered. "He's so happy and excited. He really thinks this is going to be the discovery that makes him famous."

"So?" I demanded.

"So what if it turns out to be an empty room?" Sari replied, her dark eyes watching her father. "What if grave robbers did strip the place? Or what if it isn't that prince's tomb after all? What if Daddy breaks the seal, opens the door—and finds nothing but a dusty old room filled with snakes?"

She sighed. "Daddy will be heartbroken. Just heartbroken. He's counting on this so much, Gabe. I don't know if he'll be able to take the disappointment."

"Why look on the gloomy side?" I replied. "What if—"

32

I stopped because Uncle Ben was hurrying back to us. "Let's go down to the chamber," he said excitedly. "The workers think we are very close to uncovering the tomb entrance."

He put an arm on each of our shoulders and guided us to the pyramid.

As we stepped into the shade of the pyramid, the air grew cooler. The low entrance dug at the bottom of the back wall came into view. It was just big enough for us to enter one at a time. Peering into the narrow hole, I saw that the tunnel dropped steeply.

I hope I don't fall, I thought, a heavy knot of fear tightening my stomach. I pictured myself falling and falling down an endless, dark hole.

Mainly, I didn't want to fall in front of Sari. I knew she'd never let me forget it.

Uncle Ben handed Sari and me bright yellow hard hats. They had lights built into them, like miners' hats. "Stick close together," he instructed. "I remember last summer. You two wandered off and got us into a lot of trouble."

"W-we will," I stammered. I was trying not to sound nervous, but I couldn't help it.

I glanced at Sari. She was adjusting the yellow hard hat over her hair. She seemed as calm and confident as ever.

"I'll lead the way," Uncle Ben said, pulling the chin strap under his chin. He turned and started to lower himself into the hole.

But a shrill cry from behind us made us all stop and turn around.

"Stop! Please—stop! Don't go in!"

A young woman came running across the sand. Her long, black hair flew behind her head as she ran. She carried a brown briefcase in one hand. A camera, strapped around her neck, bobbed in front of her.

She stopped in front of us and smiled at Uncle Ben. "Dr Hassad?" she asked breathlessly.

My uncle nodded. "Yes?" He waited for her to catch her breath.

Wow. She's really pretty, I thought. She had long, black hair, sleek and shiny. She had a fringe cut straight across her forehead. Beneath the fringe were the most beautiful green eyes I'd ever seen.

She was dressed all in white. A white suit jacket and a white blouse over white slacks. She was short—only an inch or two taller than Sari.

She must be a movie star or something, I told myself. She's so great-looking!

35

She set her briefcase down on the sand and brushed back her long, black hair. "I'm sorry I shouted like that, Dr Hassad," she told my uncle. "It's just that I needed to talk to you. I didn't want you to disappear into the pyramid."

Uncle Ben narrowed his eyes at her, studying her. "How did you get past the security guard?" he asked, pulling off the hard hat.

"I showed them my press card," she replied. "I'm a reporter for the Cairo *Sun*. My name is Nila Rahmad. I was hoping—"

"Nila?" Uncle Ben interrupted. "What a pretty name."

She smiled. "Yes. My mother named me after the River of Life, the Nile."

"Well, it's a very pretty name," Uncle Ben replied. His eyes twinkled. "But I'm not ready to have any reporters write about our work here."

Nila frowned and bit her lower lip. "I spoke to Dr Fielding a few days ago," she said.

My uncle's eyes widened in surprise. "You did?"

"Dr Fielding gave me permission to write about your discovery," Nila insisted, her green eyes locked on my uncle.

"Well, we haven't discovered anything yet!" Uncle Ben said sharply. "There may not be anything to discover."

"That's not what Dr Fielding told me," Nila replied. "He seemed confident that you were about to make a discovery that would shock the world."

Uncle Ben laughed. "Sometimes my partner gets excited and talks too much," he told Nila.

Nila's eyes pleaded with my uncle. "May I come into the pyramid with you?" She glanced at Sari and me. "I see you have two other visitors."

"My daughter, Sari, and my nephew, Gabe," Uncle Ben replied.

"Well, could I come down with them?" Nila pleaded. "I promise I won't write a word for my paper until you give me permission."

Uncle Ben rubbed his chin thoughtfully. He swung the hard hat back on to his head. "No photographs, either," he muttered.

"Does that mean I can come?" Nila asked excitedly.

Uncle Ben nodded. "As an observer." He was trying to act real tough. But I could see he liked her.

Nila flashed him a warm smile. "Thank you, Dr Hassad."

He reached into the storage cart and handed her a yellow hard hat. "We won't be making any amazing discoveries today," he warned her. "But we're getting very close—to something."

As she slipped on the heavy helmet, Nila turned to Sari and me. "Is this your first time in the pyramid?" she asked.

"No way. I've already been down three times," Sari boasted. "It's really awesome."

"I just arrived yesterday," I said. "So it's my first time down in—"

I stopped when I saw Nila's expression change.

Why was she staring at me like that?

I glanced down and realized that she was staring at the amber pendant. Her mouth was open in shock.

"No! I don't believe this! I really don't! This is so *weird*!" she exclaimed.

"Wh-what's wrong?" I stammered.

"We're *twins*!" Nila declared. She reached under her suit jacket and pulled out a pendant she wore around her neck.

An amber pendant, shaped exactly like mine.

"How unusual!" Uncle Ben exclaimed.

Nila grasped my pendant between her fingers and lowered her face to examine it. "You have a scarab inside yours," she told me, turning the pendant around in her fingers.

She dropped mine and held hers up for me to see. "Look, Gabe. Mine is empty."

I gazed into her pendant. It looked like clear orange glass. Nothing inside.

"I think *yours* is prettier," Sari told Nila. "I wouldn't want to wear a dead bug around my neck."

"But it's supposed to be good luck or something," Nila replied. She tucked the pendant back under her white jacket. "I hope it isn't *bad*

39

luck to have an empty one!"

"I hope so, too," Uncle Ben commented dryly. He turned and led us into the pyramid opening.

I'm not really sure how I got lost.

Sari and I were walking together behind Uncle Ben and Nila. We were close behind them. I could hear my uncle explaining about how the tunnel walls were granite and limestone.

Our helmet lights were on. The narrow beams of yellow light darted and crisscrossed over the dusty tunnel floor and walls as we made our way deeper and deeper into the pyramid.

The ceiling hung low, and we all had to stoop as we walked. The tunnel kept curving, and there were several smaller tunnels that branched off. "False starts and dead ends," Uncle Ben called them.

It was hard to see in the flickering light from our helmets. I stumbled once and scraped my elbow against the rough tunnel wall. It was surprisingly cool down here, and I wished I had worn a sweatshirt or something.

Up ahead, Uncle Ben was telling Nila about King Tut and Prince Khor-Ru. It sounded to me as if Uncle Ben was trying to impress her. I wondered if he had a crush on her or something.

"This is so thrilling!" I heard Nila exclaim. "It was so nice of Dr Fielding and you to let me see it."

40

"Who is Dr Fielding?" I whispered to Sari.

"My father's partner," Sari whispered back. "But Daddy doesn't like him. You'll probably meet him. He's always around. I don't like him much, either."

I stopped to examine a strange-looking marking on the tunnel wall. It was shaped like some kind of animal head. "Sari—look!" I whispered. "An ancient drawing."

Sari rolled her eyes. "It's Bart Simpson," she muttered. "One of Daddy's workers must have drawn it there."

"I knew that!" I lied. "I was just teasing you."

When I was going to stop making a fool of myself in front of my cousin?

I turned back from the stupid drawing on the wall—and Sari had vanished.

I could see the narrow beam of light from her hard hat up ahead. "Hey—wait up!" I called. But the light disappeared as the tunnel curved away.

And then I stumbled again.

My helmet hit the tunnel wall. And the light went out.

"Hey—Sari? Uncle Ben?" I called to them. I leaned heavily against the wall, afraid to move in the total darkness.

"Hey—! Can anybody hear me?" My voice echoed down the narrow tunnel.

But no one replied.

I pulled off the hard hat and fiddled with the

light. I turned it, trying to tighten it. Then I shook the whole hat. But the light wouldn't come back on.

Sighing, I strapped the hat back on to my head.

Now what? I thought, starting to feel a little afraid. My stomach began fluttering. My throat suddenly felt dry.

"Hey—can anybody hear me?" I shouted. "I'm in the dark back here. I can't see!"

No reply.

Where *were* they? Didn't they notice that I had disappeared?

"Well, I'll just wait right here for them," I murmured to myself.

I leaned my shoulder against the tunnel wall—and fell right through the wall.

No way to catch my balance. Nothing to grab on to.

I was falling, falling down through total darkness.

My hands flailed wildly as I fell.

I reached out frantically for something to grab on to.

It all happened too fast to cry out.

I landed hard on my back. Pain shot out through my arms and legs. The darkness swirled around me.

My breath was knocked right out of me. I saw bright flashes of red, then everything went black again. I struggled to breathe, but couldn't suck in any air.

I had that horrible heavy feeling in my chest, like when a basketball hits you in the stomach.

Finally, I sat up, struggling to see in the total darkness. I heard a soft, shuffling sound. Something scraping over the hard dirt floor.

"Hey—can anyone hear me?" My voice came out a hoarse whisper.

Now my back ached, but I was starting to breathe normally.

"Hey—I'm down here!" I called, a little louder. No reply.

Didn't they miss me? Weren't they looking for me?

I was leaning back on my hands, starting to feel better. My right hand started to itch.

I reached to scratch it and brushed something away.

And realized my legs were itching, too. And felt something crawling on my left wrist.

I shook my hand hard. "What's going on here?" I whispered to myself.

My entire body tingled. I felt soft pinpricks up my arms and legs.

Shaking both arms, I jumped to my feet. And banged my helmet against a low ledge.

The light flickered on.

I gasped when I saw the crawling creatures in the narrow beam of light.

Spiders. Hundreds of bulby, white spiders, thick on the chamber floor.

They scuttled across the floor, climbing over each other. As I jerked my head up and the light swept up with it, I saw that the stone walls were covered with them, too. The white spiders made the wall appear to move, as if it were alive.

Spiders hung on invisible threads from the chamber ceiling. They seemed to bob and float in mid-air.

I shook one off the back of my hand.

And, with a gasp, realized why my legs itched. Spiders were crawling all over them. Up over my arms. Down my back.

"Help—somebody! Please!" I managed to cry out.

I felt a spider drop on to the top of my head.

I brushed it away with a frantic slap. "Somebody—help me!" I screamed. "Can anyone hear me?"

And then I saw something scarier. Much scarier. A snake slid down from above me, lowering itself rapidly towards my face.

I ducked and tried to cover my head as the snake silently dropped towards me.

"Grab it!" I heard someone call. "Grab on to it!"

With a startled cry, I raised my eyes. The light beam followed. And I saw that it was not a snake that stretched from above—but a rope.

"Grab on to it, Gabe! Hurry!" Sari shouted urgently from high above.

Brushing away spiders, kicking frantically to shake them off my trainers, I grasped the rope with both hands.

And felt myself being tugged up, pulled up through the darkness to the tunnel floor above.

A few seconds later, Uncle Ben reached down and grabbed me under the shoulders. As he hoisted me up, I could see Sari and Nila pulling with all their might on the rope.

I cheered happily as my feet touched solid ground. But I didn't have long to celebrate. My entire body felt as if it were on fire!

I went wild, kicking my legs, brushing spiders off my arms, scratching spiders off my back, stamping on the spiders as they scuttled off me.

Glancing up, I saw that Sari was laughing at me. "Gabe, what do you call that dance?" she asked.

Uncle Ben and Nila laughed, too. "How did you fall down there, Gabe?" my uncle demanded, peering down into the spider chamber.

"The wall—it gave way," I told him, frantically scratching my legs.

"I thought you were still with me," Sari explained. "When I turned around . . ." Her voice trailed off.

The light on Uncle Ben's helmet beamed down to the lower chamber. "That's a long fall," Uncle Ben said, turning back to me. "Are you sure you're okay?"

I nodded. "Yeah. I think so. It knocked the wind out of me. And then the spiders—"

"There must be hundreds of chambers like that," my uncle commented, glancing at Nila. "The pyramid builders made a maze of tunnels and chambers—to fool tomb robbers and keep them from finding the real tomb."

"Yuck! Such fat spiders!" Sari groaned, stepping back.

"There are millions of them down there," I told

47

her. "On the walls, hanging from the ceiling—everywhere."

"This is going to give me bad dreams," Nila said softly, moving closer to Uncle Ben.

"You sure you're okay?" my uncle demanded again.

I started to reply. Then I suddenly remembered something. The mummy hand. It was tucked in my back pocket.

Had it been crushed when I landed on it?

My heart skipped a beat. I didn't want anything bad to happen to that little hand. It was my good luck charm.

I reached into my jeans pocket and pulled it out. Holding it under the light from my hard hat, I examined it carefully.

I breathed a sigh of relief when I saw that it was okay. It still felt cold. But it hadn't been crushed.

"What's that?" Nila asked, leaning closer to see it better. She brushed her long hair away from her face. "Is that The Summoner?"

"How did you know that?" I demanded, holding the hand up so she could see it better.

Nila stared at it intently. "I know a lot about ancient Egypt," she replied. "I've studied it my whole life."

"It might be an ancient relic," Uncle Ben broke in.

48

"Or it might just be a tacky souvenir," Sari added.

"It has real powers," I insisted, brushing it off carefully. "I landed on it down there—" I pointed to the spider chamber—"and it didn't get crushed."

"I guess it *is* a good luck charm," Nila said, turning back to Uncle Ben.

"Then why didn't it keep Gabe from falling through that wall?" Sari cracked.

Before I could answer, I saw the mummy hand move. The tiny fingers slowly curled. Out and then in.

I cried out and nearly dropped it.

"Gabe—now what?" Uncle Ben demanded sharply.

"Uh . . . nothing," I replied.

They wouldn't believe me anyway.

"I think we've done enough exploring for now," Uncle Ben said.

As we made our way to the entrance, I held the mummy hand in front of me.

I wasn't seeing things. I knew that for sure. The fingers really had moved.

But why?

Was the hand trying to signal to me? Was it trying to warn me about something?

Two days later, Uncle Ben's workers reached the doorway to the burial chamber.

Sari and I had spent the two days hanging around in the tent or exploring the area outside the pyramid. Since it was mostly sand, there wasn't much to explore.

We spent one long afternoon playing game after game of Scrabble. Playing Scrabble with Sari wasn't much fun at all. She is a very defensive player and spent hours figuring out ways to clog the board and block me from getting any good words.

Whenever I put down a really good word, Sari claimed it wasn't a real word and couldn't be allowed. And since we didn't have a dictionary in the tent, she won most of the arguments.

Uncle Ben, meanwhile, seemed really stressed out. I thought maybe he was nervous about finally opening the tomb.

He barely spoke to Sari and me. Instead, he

spent a lot of time meeting with people I didn't recognize. He seemed very serious and business-like. None of his usual backslapping and joking.

Uncle Ben also spent a lot of time talking to Nila. At first, she'd said she wanted to write about his discovery in the pyramid. But now she'd decided to write an article about him. She wrote down nearly every word he said in a little pad she carried with her.

Then, at breakfast, he finally smiled for the first time in two days. "Today's the day," he announced.

Sari and I couldn't hide our excitement. "Are you taking us with you?" I asked.

Uncle Ben nodded. "I want you to be there," he replied. "Perhaps we will make history today. Perhaps it will be a day you will want to remember for the rest of your lives." He shrugged and added thoughtfully: "Perhaps."

A few minutes later, the three of us followed several workers across the sand towards the pyramid. It was a grey day. Heavy clouds hovered low in the sky, threatening rain. The pyramid rose up darkly to meet the clouds.

As we approached the small opening in the back wall, Nila came running up, her camera bobbing in front of her. She wore a long-sleeved, blue denim work shirt over loose-fitting, faded jeans. Uncle Ben greeted her warmly. "But still no photographs," he told her firmly. "Promise?"

Nila smiled back at him. Her green eyes lit up excitedly. She raised a hand to her heart. "Promise."

We all took yellow hard hats from the equipment dump. Uncle Ben was carrying a large stone mallet. He lowered himself into the entrance, and we followed.

My heart was racing as I hurried to keep up with Sari. The lights from our helmets darted over the narrow tunnel. Far up ahead, I could hear the voices of workers and the steady scrape of their digging tools.

"This is really awesome!" I exclaimed breathlessly to Sari.

"Maybe the tomb is filled with jewels," Sari whispered as we made our way around a curve. "Sapphires and rubies and emeralds. Maybe I'll get to try on a jewelled crown worn by an Egyptian princess."

"Do you think there's a mummy in the tomb?" I asked. I wasn't too interested in jewels. "Do you think the mummified body of Prince Khor-Ru is lying there, waiting to be discovered?"

Sari made a disgusted face. "Is that all you can think about—mummies?"

"Well, we *are* in an ancient Egyptian pyramid!" I shot back.

"There could be millions of pounds' worth of jewels and relics in that tomb," Sari scolded.

"And all you can think about is some mouldy old body wrapped up in tar and gauze." She shook her head. "You know, most kids get over their fascination with mummies by the time they're eight or nine."

"Uncle Ben didn't!" I replied.

That shut her up.

We followed Nila and Uncle Ben in silence. After a while, the narrow tunnel curved up sharply. The air grew warmer as we followed it up.

I could see lights ahead. Two battery-powered spotlights were trained on the far wall. As we drew closer, I realized it wasn't a wall. It was a door.

Four workers—two men and two women—were on their knees, working with small shovels and picks. They were scraping the last chunks of dirt away from the door.

"It looks beautiful!" Uncle Ben cried, running up to the workers. They turned to greet him. "It's awesome in the true sense of the word!" he declared.

Nila, Sari, and I stepped up behind him. Uncle Ben was right. The ancient door really was awesome!

It wasn't very tall. I could see that Uncle Ben would have to stoop to step into it. But it looked like a door fit for a prince.

The dark mahogany wood—now petrified—

must have been brought from far away. I knew that kind of wood didn't come from any trees that grew in Egypt.

Strange hieroglyphics covered the door from top to bottom. I recognized birds, and cats, and other animals etched deeply into the dark wood.

The most startling sight of all was the seal that locked the door—a snarling lion's head, sculpted in gold. The light from the spotlights made the lion glow like the sun.

"The gold is soft," I heard one of the workers tell my uncle. "The seal will break away easily."

Uncle Ben lowered his heavy mallet to the ground. He stared for a long moment at the glowing lion's head, then turned back to us. "They thought this lion would scare any intruders away from the tomb," he explained. "I guess it worked. Till now."

"Dr Hassad, I have to photograph the actual breaking of the seal," Nila said, stepping up beside him. "You really must let me. We can't let the moment go unrecorded."

He gazed at her thoughtfully. "Well . . . okay," he agreed.

A pleased smile crossed her face as she raised her camera. "Thanks, Ben."

The workers stepped back. One of them handed Uncle Ben a hammer and a delicate tool that looked like a doctor's scalpel. "It's all yours, Dr Hassad," she said.

Uncle Ben raised the tools and stepped up to the seal. "Once I break this seal, we will open the door and step into a room that hasn't been seen in four thousand years," he announced.

Nila steadied her camera over her eye, carefully adjusting the lens.

Sari and I moved up beside the workers.

The gold lion appeared to glow brighter as Uncle Ben raised the tool. A hush fell over the tunnel. I could feel the excitement, feel the tension in the air.

Such suspense!

I realized I had been holding my breath. I let it out in a long, silent whoosh and took another.

I glanced at Sari. She was nervously chewing her lower lip. Her hands were pressed tightly at her sides.

"Anyone hungry? Maybe we should forget about this and send out for a pizza!" Uncle Ben joked.

We all laughed loudly.

That was Uncle Ben for you—cracking a dumb joke at what might be the most exciting moment of his life.

The tense silence returned. Uncle Ben's expression turned serious. He turned back to the ancient seal. He raised the small chisel to the back of the seal. Then he started to lift the hammer.

And a booming voice rang out, "PLEASE—LET ME REST IN PEACE!"

I let out a startled cry.

"LET ME REST IN PEACE!" the booming voice repeated.

I saw Uncle Ben lower his chisel. He spun around, his eyes wide with surprise.

I realized the voice came from behind us. I turned to see a man I had never seen before, half hidden in the shadowy tunnel. He made his way towards us, taking long, steady strides.

He was a tall, lanky man, so tall he really had to hunch his shoulders in the low tunnel. Bald except for a fringe of dark hair at the ears, he had a slender face, an unfriendly scowl on his thin lips.

He wore a perfectly ironed safari jacket over a shirt and tie. His black eyes, like little raisins, glared at my uncle. I wondered if the man ever ate. He was as skinny as a mummy himself!

"Omar—!" Uncle Ben started. "I wasn't expecting you back from Cairo."

"Let me rest in peace," Dr Fielding repeated, softer this time. "Those are the words of Prince Khor-Ru. Written on the ancient stone we found last month. That was the prince's wish."

"Omar, we've been over this before," my uncle replied, sighing. He lowered the hammer and chisel to his sides.

Dr Fielding pushed past Sari and me as if we weren't there. He stopped in front of my uncle and swept a hand back over his bald head.

"Well, then, how can you dare to break the seal?" Dr Fielding demanded.

"I am a scientist," my uncle replied slowly, speaking each word clearly and distinctly. "I cannot allow superstition to stand in the way of discovery, Omar."

"I am also a scientist," Dr Fielding replied, using both hands to tighten his tie. "But I am not willing to defile this ancient tomb. I am not willing to go against the wishes of Prince Khor-Ru. And I am not willing to call the words of the hieroglyph mere superstition."

"This is where we disagree," Uncle Ben said softly. He motioned to the four workers. "We have spent too many months, too many years, to stop just outside the door. We have come this far, Omar. We must go the rest of the way."

Dr Fielding chewed his lower lip. He pointed to the top of the door. "Look, Ben. There are the same hieroglyphs as on the stone. The same warning. *Let me rest in peace.*"

"I know, I know," my uncle said, frowning.

"The warning is very clear," Dr Fielding continued heatedly, his tiny raisin eyes narrowed at my uncle. "If anyone should disturb the prince, if anyone should repeat the ancient words written on the tomb five times—the mummified prince shall come to life. And he shall seek his vengeance on those who disturbed him."

Listening to those words made me shudder. I stared hard at Uncle Ben. Why hadn't he ever told Sari and me about the prince's threat? Why hadn't he ever mentioned the words of warning they had found on an ancient stone?

Was he afraid he might frighten us?

Was he frightened himself?

No. No way.

He didn't seem at all frightened now as he argued with Dr Fielding. I could tell they had had this argument before. And I could see there was no way that Dr Fielding was going to stop my uncle from breaking the seal and entering the tomb.

"This is my final warning, Ben—" Dr Fielding said. "For the sake of everyone here . . ." He motioned with one hand to the four workers.

59

"Superstition," Uncle Ben replied. "I cannot be stopped by superstition. I am a scientist." He raised the chisel and hammer. "The seal will be broken."

Dr Fielding tossed up both hands in disgust. "I will not be a party to this," he declared. He spun round, nearly hitting his head on the tunnel ceiling. Then, muttering to himself, he hurried away, disappearing quickly into the darkness of the tunnel.

Uncle Ben took a couple of steps after him. "Omar—? Omar?"

But we could hear Dr Fielding's footsteps growing fainter as he made his way out of the pyramid.

Uncle Ben sighed and leaned close to me. "I don't trust that man," he muttered. "He doesn't really care about the old superstitions. He wants to steal this discovery for himself. That's why he tried to make me stop outside the door."

I didn't know how to reply. My uncle's words startled me. I thought scientists had rules about who took credit for what discoveries.

Uncle Ben whispered something to Nila. Then he made his way back to the four workers. "If any of you agree with Dr Fielding," he told them, "you are free to leave now."

The workers exchanged glances with one another.

"You have all heard the words of warning on

the tomb door. I do not want to force anyone to enter the tomb," Uncle Ben told them.

"But we have worked so hard," one of the men said. "We cannot stop here. We have no choice. We *have* to open that door."

A smile crossed my uncle's face. "I agree," he said, turning back to the lion seal.

I glanced at Sari and realized that she was already staring at me. "Gabe, if you're scared, Daddy will let you leave," she whispered. "You don't have to be embarrassed."

She never quits!

"I'm staying," I whispered back. "But if you want me to walk you back to the tent, I will."

A loud *clink* made us both turn back to the door. Uncle Ben was working to prise off the gold lion seal. Nila had her camera poised. The workers stood tensely, watching Uncle Ben's every move.

Uncle Ben worked slowly, carefully. He slid the chisel behind the ancient seal and gently prised and scraped.

A few minutes later, the seal fell into my uncle's hands. Nila busily snapped photograph after photograph. Uncle Ben carefully passed it to one of the workers. "That's not a Christmas gift," he joked. "I'm keeping that for my mantelpiece!"

Everyone laughed.

Uncle Ben gripped the edge of the door with both hands. "I'm going in first," he announced. "If I'm not back in twenty minutes, go and tell Dr Fielding he was right!"

More laughter.

Two of the workers moved to help Uncle Ben slide open the door. They pressed their shoulders against it, straining hard.

The door didn't budge.

"It might need a little oiling," Uncle Ben joked. "After all, it's been closed for four thousand years."

They worked for several minutes with picks and chisels, carefully freeing the door. Then they tried once again, pressing their shoulders against the heavy mahogany door.

"Yes!" Uncle Ben cried out as the door slid an inch.

Then another inch. Another inch.

Everyone pressed forward, eager to get a view of the ancient tomb.

Two of the workers moved the large spotlights, aiming them into the doorway.

As Uncle Ben and his two helpers pushed against the door, Sari and I stepped up beside Nila. "Isn't this amazing!" Nila cried excitedly. "I can't believe I'm the only reporter here! I'm so lucky!"

I'm lucky, too, I realized. How many kids would give anything to be standing right where

I am? How many kids would *love* to be one of the first people in the world to step into a four-thousand-year-old tomb in an Egyptian pyramid?

The faces of some of my friends back home suddenly popped into my mind. I realized I couldn't *wait* to tell them about my adventure here!

The door scraped noisily against the dirt floor. Another inch. Another inch.

The opening was almost big enough for a person to squeeze through.

"Move the light a little," Uncle Ben instructed. "Another few inches, and we can go in and shake hands with the prince."

The door scraped open another inch. With a great heave, Uncle Ben and his helpers forced it open another few inches.

"Yes!" he cried happily.

Nila snapped a photograph.

We all pressed forward eagerly.

Uncle Ben slid through the opening first.

Sari bumped me out of the way and cut in front of me.

My heart was pounding hard. My hands were suddenly ice cold.

I didn't care who went in first. I just wanted to go in!

One by one, we slipped into the ancient chamber.

Finally, my turn came. I took a deep breath, slipped through the opening, and saw—

—nothing.

Except for a lot of cobwebs, the chamber was bare.

Totally bare.

I let out a long sigh. Poor Uncle Ben. All that work for nothing. I felt so disappointed.

I glanced around the bare chamber. The spot-lights made the thick cobwebs glow like silver. Our shadows stretched across the dirt floor like ghosts.

I turned to Uncle Ben, expecting him to be disappointed, too. But to my surprise, he had a smile on his face. "Move the lights," he told one of the workers. "And bring the tools. We have another seal to remove."

He pointed across the empty room to the back wall. In the grey light, I could make out the outline of the door. Another sculpted lion sealed it shut.

"I *knew* this wasn't the real burial chamber!" Sari cried, grinning at me.

"As I said, the Egyptians often did this," Uncle Ben explained. "They built several false chambers to hide the real chamber from grave

65

robbers." He pulled off his hard hat and scratched his hair. "In fact," he continued, "we may find several empty chambers before we find Prince Khor-Ru's resting place."

Nila snapped a photo of Uncle Ben examining the newly discovered door. She smiled at me. "You should have seen the expression on your face, Gabe," she said. "You looked so disappointed."

"I thought—" I started. But the scrape of Uncle Ben's chisel against the seal made me stop.

We all turned to watch him work at the seal. Staring across the cobweb-filled chamber, I tried to imagine what waited for us on the other side of the door.

Another empty chamber? Or a four-thousand-year-old Egyptian prince, surrounded by all of his treasures and belongings?

Work on the door went slowly. We all broke for lunch and then returned. That afternoon Uncle Ben and his helpers worked for another couple of hours, carefully trying to remove the seal without damaging it.

As they worked, Sari and I sat on the floor and watched. The air was hot and a bit sour. I suppose it was ancient air. Sari and I talked about last summer and the adventures we'd had in the Great Pyramid. Nila snapped our picture.

"Almost got it," Uncle Ben announced.

We all started to get excited again. Sari and I climbed to our feet and crossed the room to get a better view.

The lion seal slid free from the door. Two of the workers placed it gently into a padded crate. Then Uncle Ben and the other two workers set to work pushing open the door.

This door proved even more difficult than the last. "It's . . . really . . . stuck," Uncle Ben groaned. He and the workers pulled out more tools and began prising and chipping away the hard crust that had formed on the doorway over the centuries.

An hour later, they got the door to slide an inch. Then another inch. Another.

When it had slid halfway open, Uncle Ben removed the light from his helmet and beamed it through the opening. He peered into the next chamber for the longest time without saying a word.

Sari and I moved closer. My heart began racing again.

What did he see? I wondered. What was he staring at so silently?

Finally, Uncle Ben lowered the light and turned back to us. "We've made a big mistake," he said quietly.

A shocked silence fell over the room. I swallowed hard, stunned by my uncle's words.

But then a broad smile crossed his face. "We made a mistake by underestimating our discovery!" he exclaimed. "This will be more important than the discovery of King Tut! This tomb is even grander!"

A gleeful cheer echoed against the stone walls. The workers rushed forward to shake Uncle Ben's hand and offer their congratulations.

"Congratulations to us all!" Uncle Ben declared happily.

We were all laughing and talking excitedly as we slipped through the narrow opening, into the next chamber.

As the lights beamed over the vast room, I knew I was seeing something I would never forget. Even the thick layer of dust and cobwebs could not cover the amazing treasures that filled the chamber.

My eyes darted quickly around. I struggled to focus on it all. But there was too much to see! I actually felt dizzy.

The walls were covered from floor to ceiling with hieroglyphics, etched into the stone. The floor was cluttered with furniture and other objects. It looked more like someone's attic or a storeroom than a tomb!

A tall, straight-backed throne caught my eye. It had a golden, radiating sun etched into the seatback. Behind it, I saw chairs and benches, and a long couch.

Against the wall were stacked dozens of stone and clay jars. Some were cracked and broken. But many were in perfect condition.

A gold monkey's head lay on its side in the middle of the floor. Behind it, I saw several large chests.

Uncle Ben and one of the workers carefully pulled back the lid of one of the chests. Their eyes grew wide as they gaped inside.

"Jewellery!" Uncle Ben declared. "It's filled with gold jewellery!"

Sari came up beside me, an excited grin on her face.

"This is *awesome*!" I whispered.

She nodded agreement. "Awesome!"

We whispered in the heavy silence. No one else talked. Everyone was too overwhelmed by the amazing sight. The loudest sound was the clicking of Nila's camera.

Uncle Ben stepped between Sari and me and placed a hand on our shoulders. "Isn't this unbelievable?" he cried. "It's all in perfect condition. Untouched for four thousand years."

When I glanced up at him, I saw that he had tears in his eyes. This is the greatest moment of Uncle Ben's life, I realized.

"We must be very careful—" Uncle Ben started. But he stopped in mid-sentence, and I saw his expression change.

As he guided Sari and me across the room, I saw what he was staring at. A large stone mummy case, hidden in shadow, stood against the far wall.

"Oh, wow!" I murmured as we stepped up to it.

Made of smooth, grey stone, the heavy lid had a long crack down the centre.

"Is the prince buried inside it?" Sari asked eagerly.

It took Uncle Ben a moment to reply. He stood between us, his eyes locked on the ancient mummy case. "We'll soon see," he finally replied.

As he and the four workers struggled to move the lid, Nila lowered her camera and stepped forward to watch. Her green eyes stared intensely as the lid slowly slid away.

Inside was a coffin in the shape of the mummy. It wasn't very long. And it was narrower than I thought it would be.

The workers slowly prised open the coffin's lid. I gasped and grabbed Uncle Ben's hand as the mummy was revealed.

It looked so tiny and frail!

"Prince Khor-Ru," Uncle Ben muttered, staring down into the stone case.

The prince lay on his back, his slender arms crossed over his chest. Black tar had seeped through the bandages. The gauze had worn away from the head, revealing the tar-covered skull.

As I leaned over the case, my heart in my throat, the tar-blackened eyes seemed to stare helplessly up at me.

There's a real person inside there, I thought, feeling a chill run down my spine. He's about my size. And he died. And they covered him with hot tar and cloth. And he's been lying in this case for four thousand years.

A real person. A royal prince.

I stared at the stained, cracked tar that covered his face. At the gauze-like cloth, all frayed and yellowed. At the stiff body, so frail and small.

He was alive once, I thought. Did he ever dream that four thousand years later, people would open his coffin and stare at him? Stare at his mummified body?

71

I took a step back to catch my breath. It was *too* exciting.

I saw that Nila also had tears in her eyes. She rested both hands on the edge of the case and leaned over the prince's body, her eyes locked on the blackened face.

"These may be the best-preserved remains ever found," Uncle Ben said quietly. "Of course we will have to do many tests to determine the young man's identity. But, judging from everything else in this chamber, I think it's safe to say . . ."

His voice trailed off as we all heard sounds from the outer chamber. Footsteps. Voices.

I spun around towards the doorway as four black-uniformed police officers burst into the room. "Okay. Everybody take one step back," one of them ordered, lowering his hand to the gun holster at his side.

Startled cries filled the room. Uncle Ben spun
round, his eyes wide with surprise. "What is
happening?" he cried.

The four Cairo police officers, their features
set in hard frowns, moved quietly into the centre
of the room.

"Be careful!" Uncle Ben warned, standing
in front of the mummy case as if protecting
it. "Do not move anything. It is all terribly
fragile."

He pulled off the hard hat. His eyes went
from officer to officer. "What are you doing
here?"

"I asked them to come," a voice boomed from
the doorway.

Dr Fielding entered, a pleased expression on
his face. His tiny eyes danced excitedly.

"Omar—I don't understand," Uncle Ben
said, taking a few steps towards the other
scientist.

"I thought it best to protect the contents of the room," Dr Fielding replied. He gazed quickly around the room, taking in the treasures. "Wonderful! This is wonderful!" he cried. He stepped forward and shook my uncle's hand enthusiastically. "Congratulations, everyone!" he boomed. "This is almost too much to believe."

Uncle Ben's expression softened. "I still do not understand the need for them," he said, motioning to the grim-faced officers. "No one in this room is about to steal anything."

"Certainly not," Dr Fielding replied, still squeezing Uncle Ben's hand. "Certainly not. But word will soon get out, Ben. And I thought we should be prepared to guard what we have found."

Uncle Ben eyed the four officers suspiciously. But then he shrugged his broad shoulders. "Perhaps you are right," he told Dr Fielding. "Perhaps you are being sensible."

"Just ignore them," Dr Fielding replied. He slapped my uncle on the back. "I owe you an apology, Ben. I was wrong to try to stop you before. As a scientist, I should have known better. We owed it to the world to open this tomb. I hope you'll forgive me. We have much to celebrate—don't we!"

"I don't trust him," Uncle Ben confided that

74

evening as we walked from the tent to dinner. "I don't trust my partner at all."

It was a clear night, surprisingly cool. The purple sky was dotted with a million twinkling white stars. A steady breeze made the palm trees sway on the horizon. The big campfire up ahead dipped and shifted with the wind.

"Is Dr Fielding coming with us to dinner?" Sari asked. She wore a pale green sweater, pulled down over black leggings.

Uncle Ben shook his head. "No, he hurried to phone Cairo. I think he's eager to tell our backers the good news."

"He seemed really excited when he saw the mummy and everything," I said, glancing at the pyramid rising darkly to the evening sky.

"Yes, he did," my uncle admitted. "He certainly changed his mind in a hurry! But I'm keeping my eye on him. Omar would like nothing better than to take over the project. I'm going to keep an eye on those police officers of his, too."

"Daddy, this should be a happy night," Sari scolded. "Let's not talk about Dr Fielding. Let's just talk about Prince Khor-Ru and how you're going to be rich and famous!"

Uncle Ben laughed. "It's a deal," he told her.

Nila was waiting for us by the campfire. Uncle

Ben had invited her to join us for a barbecue. She was wearing a white sweatshirt over loose-fitting jeans. Her amber pendant caught the light from the half-moon, just rising over the tents.

She looked really pretty. She flashed Uncle Ben a warm smile as we came near. I could tell by his face that he liked her.

"Sari, you're taller than Gabe, aren't you!" Nila commented.

Sari grinned. She loved being taller than me, even though I'm a little older.

"Less than an inch," I said quickly.

"People are definitely getting taller," Nila said to my uncle. "Prince Khor-Ru was so short. He'd be a midget today!"

"It makes you wonder why such short people built such tall pyramids," Uncle Ben said, grinning.

Nila smiled and took his arm.

Sari and I exchanged glances. I could see what Sari was thinking. Her expression said: What's up with those two?

We had a great dinner. Uncle Ben burned the hamburger rolls a little. But no one really minded.

Sari downed two hamburgers. I could only eat one. That gave her something else to boast about.

I was really getting fed up with my bragging

cousin. I found myself trying to think of a way to get back at her.

Nila and Uncle Ben kidded around a lot.

"That burial chamber looked like a film set," Nila teased my uncle. "It was all too perfect. All that gold. And that perfect little mummy. It's all a fake. That's what I'm going to write in my article."

Uncle Ben laughed. He turned to me. "Did you check out the mummy, Gabe? Was this one wearing a wristwatch?"

I shook my head. "No wristwatch."

"See?" Uncle Ben told Nila. "No wristwatch. So it's *got* to be real!"

"I guess that proves it," Nila said, smiling warmly at my uncle.

"Daddy, do you know the words to bring the mummy to life?" Sari broke in. "You know. The words on the tomb that Dr Fielding was talking about?"

Uncle Ben swallowed the last bite of his hamburger. He wiped the grease off his chin with a napkin. "I can't believe that a serious scientist would believe such superstition," he murmured.

"But what *are* the six words to bring the mummy to life?" Nila demanded. "Come on, Ben. Tell us."

Uncle Ben's smile faded. He shook his finger at Nila. "Oh, no!" he declared. "I don't trust you.

If I tell you the words, you'll bring the mummy back to life just to get a good photograph for your newspaper!"

We all laughed.

We were sitting around the campfire, its orange light flickering over our faces. Uncle Ben set his plate down on the ground and spread his hands over the fire.

"*Teki Kahru Teki Kahra Teki Khari!*" he chanted in a deep voice, waving his hands over the flames.

The fire crackled. A twig made a loud popping sound that made my heart skip a beat.

"Are those the secret words?" Sari demanded.

Uncle Ben nodded solemnly. "Those are the words of the hieroglyphs over the entrance to the tomb."

"So maybe the mummy just sat up and stretched?" Sari asked.

"I'd be very surprised," Uncle Ben replied, climbing to his feet. "You're forgetting, Sari—you have to chant the words five times."

"Oh." Sari stared thoughtfully into the fire.

I repeated the words in my mind. "*Teki Kahru Teki Kahra Teki Khari!*" I needed to memorize the words. I had a plan to scare Sari.

"Where are you going?" Nila asked my uncle.

"To the communications tent," he replied. "I have to make a phone call." He turned and made his way quickly over the sand towards the row of canvas tents.

Nila let out a surprised laugh. "He didn't even say good night."

"Daddy's always like that," Sari explained, "when he has something on his mind."

"Guess I'd better go, too," Nila said, climbing to her feet and brushing sand off her jeans. "I'm going to start writing my story for the paper."

She said good night and walked quickly away, her sandals making a slapping sound against the sand.

Sari and I sat staring into the crackling fire. The half-moon had floated high in the sky. Its pale light reflected off the top of the pyramid in the distance.

"Nila is right," I told Sari. "It really did look like a film set in there."

Sari didn't reply. She stared into the fire without blinking, thinking hard. Something in the fire popped again. The sound seemed to snap her out of her thoughts.

"Do you think Nila likes Daddy?" she asked me, her dark eyes locking on mine.

"Yeah, I think so," I replied. "She's always giving him this smile." I imitated Nila's smile. "And she's always kind of teasing him."

Sari thought about my reply. "And do you think Daddy likes her?"

I grinned. "For sure." I stood up. I was eager to get back to the tent. I wanted to scare Sari.

We walked towards the tents in silence. I guessed that Sari was still thinking about her dad and Nila.

The night air was cool, but it was warm inside the tent. Moonlight filtered through the canvas. Sari pulled her trunk out from under her camp bed and got down on her knees to search through her clothes.

"Sari," I whispered. "Dare me to recite the ancient words five times?"

"Huh?" She gazed up from the trunk.

"I'm going to chant the words five times," I told her. "You know. See if anything happens."

I expected her to beg me not to. I expected her to get scared and plead: "Please, Gabe—don't do it! Don't! It's too dangerous!"

But, instead, Sari turned back to her clothes trunk. "Hey. Give it a try," she told me.

"You sure?" I asked her.

"Yeah. Why not?" she replied, pulling out a pair of denim cut-offs.

I stared across the tent at her. Was that fear I saw in her eyes? Was she just pretending to be so casual about it?

Yes. I think Sari was a little scared. And trying hard not to show it.

I took a few steps closer and chanted the ancient words, in the same low voice Uncle Ben

80

had used: *"Teki Kahru Teki Kahra Teki Khari!"*

Sari dropped the jeans and turned to watch me.

I repeated the chant a second time. *"Teki Kahru Teki Kahra Teki Khari!"*

A third time.

A fourth time.

I hesitated. I felt a cold breeze tingle the back of my neck.

Should I chant the words again? Should I go for number five?

I stared down at Sari.

She had closed the trunk lid and was leaning on it tensely, staring back at me. I could see that she was frightened. She chewed her bottom lip.

Should I chant the words for a fifth time?

I felt another chill at the back of my neck.

It's just superstition, I told myself. Four-thousand-year-old superstition.

There's no way that mouldy old mummified prince is going to come back to life just because I recite six words I don't even know the meaning of!

No way.

I suddenly thought of all the old films I had watched about mummies in ancient Egypt. In the films, the scientists always ignored ancient curses warning them not to disturb the mummies' tombs. Then the mummies always came to life to get their revenge. They staggered around, grabbed the scientists by the throat, and strangled them.

Stupid films. But I loved them.

Now, staring down at Sari, I saw that she was really scared.

I took a deep breath. I suddenly realized that I felt scared, too.

But it was too late. I had gone too far. I couldn't chicken out now.

"*Teki Kahru Teki Kahra Teki Khari!*" I shouted. The fifth time.

I froze—and waited. I don't know what I expected. A flash of lightning, maybe.

Sari climbed to her feet. She tugged at a strand of dark hair.

"Admit it. You're totally freaked," I said, unable to keep a grin from spreading across my face.

"No way!" she insisted. "Go ahead, Gabe. Chant the words again. Chant them a hundred times! You're not going to scare me! No way!"

But we both gasped when we suddenly saw a dark shadow roll over the tent wall.

And my heart completely stopped when a hoarse voice whispered into the tent: "*Are you in there?*"

My legs trembled as I stumbled back, closer to
Sari.

I could see her eyes go wide with surprise—
and fear.

The shadow moved quickly towards the tent
opening.

We had no time to scream. No time to call for
help.

Gaping into the darkness, I saw the flap
pull open—and a smooth head poked into the
tent.

"Ohhh." I let out a terrified moan as the dark
figure slumped towards us.

The mummy is alive! The horrifying thought
swept through my mind as I backed away. *The
mummy is alive!*

"Dr Fielding!" Sari cried.

"Huh?" I squinted to see better.

Yes. It was Dr Fielding.

I struggled to say hello. But my heart was

pounding so hard, I couldn't speak. I took a long, deep breath and held it.

"I'm looking for your father," Dr Fielding told Sari. "I must see him at once. It's extremely urgent."

"He—he's making a phone call," Sari replied in a shaky voice.

Dr Fielding spun round and ducked out of the tent. The flap snapped shut behind him.

I turned to Sari, my heart still pounding. "He scared me to death!" I confessed. "I thought he was in Cairo. When he poked that skinny, bald head into the tent . . ."

Sari laughed. "He really looks like a mummy—doesn't he?" Her smile faded. "I wonder why he's in such a hurry to see Daddy."

"Let's follow him!" I urged. The idea just popped into my head.

"Yes! Let's go!" I hadn't expected Sari to agree so quickly. But she was already pushing open the tent flap.

I followed her out of the tent. The night had grown cooler. A steady wind made all of the tents appear to shiver.

"Which way did he go?" I whispered.

Sari pointed. "I think that's the communications tent at the end." She started jogging across the sand.

As we ran, the wind blew sand against our legs. I heard music and voices from one of the tents. The workers were celebrating the day's discovery.

The moon cast a strip of light like a carpet along our path. Up ahead, I could see Dr Fielding's lanky body, leaning forward, lurching awkwardly towards the last tent.

He disappeared round the side of it. Sari and I stopped a few tents away. We ducked out of the moonlight, into deep shadows where we wouldn't be seen.

I could hear Dr Fielding's booming voice coming from the communications tent. He was talking rapidly, excitedly.

"What is he saying?" Sari whispered.

I couldn't make out the words.

A few seconds later, two figures emerged from the tent. Carrying bright torches, they crossed the strip of yellow moonlight, then moved quickly into shadow.

Dr Fielding appeared to be pulling Uncle Ben, pulling him towards the pyramid.

"What's going on?" Sari whispered, grabbing my sleeve. "Is he *forcing* Daddy to go with him?"

The wind swirled the sand around us. I shivered.

The two men were talking at the same time, shouting and gesturing with their torches. They're arguing about something, I realized.

Dr Fielding had a hand on Uncle Ben's

shoulder. Was he shoving Uncle Ben towards the pyramid? Or was Uncle Ben actually leading the way?

It was impossible to tell.

"Let's go," I whispered to Sari.

We stepped away from the tent and started to follow them. We walked slowly, keeping them in view, but being careful not to get too close.

"If they turn back, they'll see us," Sari whispered, huddling close to me as we crept over the sand.

She was right. There were no trees or bushes to hide behind here on the open desert.

"Maybe they won't turn back," I replied hopefully.

We crept closer. The pyramid rose up darkly in front of us.

We saw Dr Fielding and Uncle Ben stop at the opening in the side. I could hear their excited voices, but the wind carried away their words. They still seemed to be arguing.

Uncle Ben disappeared into the pyramid first. Dr Fielding went in right behind him.

"Did he shove Daddy in?" Sari demanded in a shrill, frightened voice. "It looked like he pushed him inside!"

"I—I don't know," I stammered.

We made our way closer to the entrance. Then we both stopped and stared into the darkness.

I knew we were both thinking the same thing. I knew we both had the same questions on our lips.

Should we follow them in?

Sari and I exchanged glances.

The pyramid seemed so much bigger at night, so much darker. The gusting wind howled around its walls, as if warning us to stay back.

We crept behind a pile of stones left by the workers. "Let's wait here for Daddy to come out," Sari suggested.

I didn't argue with her. We had no torches, no light of any kind. I didn't think we'd get very far wandering the dark tunnels by ourselves.

I pressed up against the smooth stones and stared at the pyramid opening. Sari gazed up at the half-moon. Thin wisps of cloud floated over it. The ground darkened in front of us.

"You don't think Daddy is in any kind of trouble, do you?" Sari asked. "I mean, he told us he didn't trust Dr Fielding. And then—"

"I'm sure Uncle Ben is okay," I told her. "I mean, Dr Fielding is a scientist. He's not a *criminal* or anything."

"But why did he force Daddy into the pyramid in the middle of the night?" Sari asked shrilly. "And what were they arguing about?"

I shrugged in reply. I didn't remember ever seeing Sari so frightened. Normally, I would have enjoyed it. She always bragged about how brave and fearless she was—especially compared to me.

But there was no way I could enjoy this. Mainly because I was just as scared as she was!

It *did* look as if the two scientists were fighting. And it *did* look as if Dr Fielding pushed Uncle Ben down into the pyramid.

Sari crossed her arms over her sweater again and narrowed her eyes at the opening. The wind fluttered her hair, blowing strands across her forehead. But she made no attempt to brush them away.

"What could be so important?" she demanded. "Why did they have to go into the pyramid now? Do you think something was stolen? Aren't those police officers from Cairo down there guarding the place?"

"I saw the four policemen leave," I told her. "They piled into their little car and drove away, just before dinner. I don't know why. Maybe they were called back to the city."

"I—I'm just confused," Sari admitted. "And worried. I didn't like the look on Dr Fielding's face. I didn't like the way he was so rude, just bursting into the tent like that. Scaring us to death. Not even saying hi."

"Calm down, Sari," I said softly. "Let's just wait. Everything will be okay."

She let out a sigh, but didn't say anything in reply.

We waited in silence. I don't know how much time went by. It seemed like hours and hours.

The shivers of cloud drifted away from the moon. The wind continued to howl eerily around the side of the pyramid.

"Where *are* they? What are they *doing* in there?" Sari demanded.

I started to reply—but stopped when I saw a flicker of light at the pyramid opening.

I grabbed Sari's arm. "Look—!" I whispered.

The light grew brighter. A figure emerged, pulling himself out quickly.

Dr Fielding.

As he stepped into the moonlight, I caught the strange expression on his face. His tiny black eyes were wide and seemed to be rolling around crazily in his head. His eyebrows twitched. His mouth was twisted open. He seemed to be breathing hard.

Dr Fielding brushed himself off with his hands and began walking away from the pyramid. He was half-walking, half-staggering, taking long quick strides with his lanky legs.

"But—where's Daddy?" Sari whispered.

Leaning out from the rocks, I could see the pyramid opening clearly. No light flickered. No sign of Uncle Ben.

"He—he isn't coming out!" Sari stammered.

And before I could react, Sari leaped out from our hiding place behind the stones—and stepped into Dr Fielding's path.

"Dr Fielding," she cried loudly, "where is my dad?"

I pushed myself away from the stones and hurried after Sari. I could see Dr Fielding's eyes spinning wildly. He didn't answer her question.

"Where is my dad?" Sari repeated shrilly.

Dr Fielding acted as if he didn't see Sari. He stepped past her, walking stiffly, awkwardly, his arms straight down.

"Dr Fielding—?" Sari called after him.

He hurried through the darkness towards the row of tents.

Sari turned back to me, her features tight with fear. "He's done something to Daddy!" she cried. "I *know* he has!"

I turned back to the pyramid opening. Still dark and silent.

The only sound now was the howling of the wind around the stone pyramid wall.

"Dr Fielding totally ignored me!" Sari cried, her face revealing her anger. "He stormed past me as if I weren't here!"

"I—I know," I stammered weakly.

"And did you see the look on his face?" she demanded. "So evil. So totally evil!"

"Sari—" I started. "Maybe—"

"Gabe, we have to go and find Daddy!" Sari interrupted. She grabbed my arm and started pulling me to the pyramid opening. "Hurry!"

"No, Sari, wait!" I insisted, tugging out of her grasp. "We can't go stumbling around the pyramid in the dark. We'll just get lost. We'll never find Uncle Ben!"

"We'll go back to the tent and get lights,"

she replied. "Quick, Gabe—"

I raised a hand to stop her. "Wait here, Sari," I instructed. "Watch for your dad. Chances are, he'll be climbing out in a few moments. I'll run and get some torches."

Staring at the dark opening, she started to argue. But then she changed her mind and agreed to my plan.

My heart pounding, I ran all the way back to the tent. I stopped at the tent opening, and gazed down the row of tents, searching for Dr Fielding.

No sign of him.

In the tent, I grabbed up two torches. Then I went hurtling back to the pyramid. *Please*, I begged silently as I ran. *Please be out of the pyramid, Uncle Ben. Please be safe.*

But as I frantically made my way over the sand, I could see Sari standing by herself. Even from a distance, I could see her frightened expression as she paced tensely back and forth in front of the pyramid opening.

Uncle Ben, where are you? I wondered. Why haven't you come out of the pyramid? Are you okay?

Sari and I didn't say a word. There was no need.

We clicked on the torches, then made our way into the pyramid opening. It seemed much steeper than I remembered. I nearly lost my balance, lowering myself to the tunnel floor.

Our lights crisscrossed over the dirt floor. I raised mine to the low ceiling. Keeping the light high, I led the way through the curving tunnel.

Creeping along slowly, I trailed one hand against the wall to steady myself. The wall felt soft and crumbly. Sari kept on my heels, her bright beam of light playing over the floor in front of our feet.

She stopped suddenly as the tunnel curved into a small, empty chamber. "How do we know we're going in the right direction?" she asked, her voice a quivering whisper.

I shrugged, breathing hard. "I thought you knew your way," I murmured.

"I've only been down here with Daddy," she replied, her eyes over my shoulders, searching the empty chamber.

"We'll keep going until we find him," I told her, forcing myself to sound braver than I felt.

She stepped in front of me, shining the light over the chamber walls. "Daddy!" she shouted. "Daddy? Can you hear me?"

Her voice echoed down the tunnel. Even the echo sounded frightened.

We froze in place and listened for a reply.

Silence.

"Come on," I urged. I had to lower my head to step into the next narrow tunnel.

Where did it lead? Were we heading towards Prince Khor-Ru's tomb? Is that where we would find Uncle Ben?

Questions, questions. I tried to stop them from coming. But they filled my mind, pestering me, repeating, echoing in my head, as we followed the tunnel's curves.

"Daddy? Daddy—where *are* you?" Sari's cries became more frantic as we moved deeper and deeper into the pyramid.

The tunnel curved up steeply, then levelled off. Sari suddenly stopped. Startled, I bumped into her hard, nearly making her drop her torch. "Sorry," I whispered.

"Gabe, look—!" she cried, pointing her beam of light just ahead of her trainers. "Foot-prints!"

I lowered my eyes to the small circle of light. I could see a set of bootprints in the dirt. A heel and spiky bumps. "Work boots," I muttered.

She circled the floor with the light. There were several different prints in the dirt, heading in the same direction we were.

"Does this mean we're going the right way?" she asked.

"Maybe," I replied, studying the prints. "It's hard to tell whether these are new or old."

"Daddy?" Sari shouted eagerly. "Can you hear me?"

No reply.

She frowned and motioned for me to follow. Seeing the many sets of prints gave us new hope, and we moved faster, trailing our hands along the wall to steady ourselves as we made our way.

We both cried out happily when we realized we had reached the outer chamber to the tomb. Our lights played over the ancient hieroglyphs that covered the wall and the doorway.

"Daddy? Daddy?" Sari's voice cut through the heavy silence.

We darted through the empty chamber, then slipped through the opening that led to the tomb. The prince's burial chamber stretched out in front of us, dark and silent.

"Daddy? Daddy?" Sari tried again.

I shouted, too. "Uncle Ben? Are you here?"

Silence.

I swept my light over the room's clutter of treasures, over the heavy chests, the chairs, the clay jars piled in the corner.

"He isn't here," Sari choked out with a disappointed sob.

"Then where did Dr Fielding bring Uncle Ben?" I asked, thinking out loud. "There's nowhere else in the pyramid that they might come."

Sari's light came to rest on the large stone mummy case. Her eyes narrowed as she studied it.

"Uncle Ben!" I shouted frantically. "Are you in here somewhere?"

Sari grabbed my arm. "Gabe—look!" she cried. Her light remained on the mummy case.

I couldn't work out what she was trying to show me. "What about it?" I demanded.

"The lid," Sari murmured.

I gazed at the lid. The heavy stone slab covered the case tightly.

"The lid is closed," Sari continued, stepping away from me and towards the mummy case. Her light remained on the lid.

"Yeah. So?" I still didn't understand.

"When we all left this afternoon," Sari explained, "the lid was open. In fact, I remember Daddy telling the workers to leave the lid open for tonight."

"You're right!" I cried.

"Help me, Gabe," Sari pleaded, putting her torch down at her feet. "We have to open the mummy case."

I hesitated for a second, feeling a wave of cold fear run down my body. Then I took a deep breath and moved to help Sari.

She was already pushing the stone lid with both hands. I stepped up beside her and pushed, too. Pushed with all my might.

The stone slab slid more easily than I'd guessed.

Working together, Sari and I strained against the lid, pushing . . . pushing.

We moved it about a foot.

Then we both lowered our heads to peer into the mummy case—and gasped in horror.

"Daddy!" Sari shrieked.

Uncle Ben lay on his back, knees raised, hands at his sides, his eyes shut. Sari and I shoved the heavy stone lid open another foot.

"Is he—? Is he—?" Sari stammered.

I pressed my hand on his chest. His heart was thumping with a steady beat. "He's breathing," I told her.

I leaned into the mummy case. "Uncle Ben? Can you hear me? Uncle Ben?"

He didn't move.

I lifted his hand and squeezed it. It felt warm, but limp. "Uncle Ben? Wake up!" I shouted.

His eyes didn't open. I lowered the hand back to the bottom of the mummy case. "He's out cold," I murmured.

Sari stood behind me, both hands pressed against her cheeks. She stared down at Uncle Ben, her eyes wide with fear. "I—I don't believe this!" she cried in a tiny voice. "Dr Fielding left

100

Daddy here to suffocate! If we hadn't come along . . ." Her voice trailed off.

Uncle Ben let out a low groan.

Sari and I stared down at him hopefully. But he didn't open his eyes.

"We have to call the police," I told Sari. "We have to tell them about Dr Fielding."

"But we can't just leave Daddy here," Sari replied.

I started to reply—but a frightening thought burst into my mind. I felt a shudder of fear roll down my body. "Sari?" I started. "If Uncle Ben is lying in the mummy case . . . then where is the mummy?"

Her mouth dropped open. She stared back at me in stunned silence.

And then we both heard the footsteps.

Slow, scraping footsteps.

And saw the mummy stagger stiffly into the room.

I opened my mouth to scream—but no sound came out.

The mummy lurched stiffly through the chamber doorway. He stared straight ahead with his vacant, tarry eyes. Under the ancient layers of tar, the skull grinned at us.

Scrape. Scrape.

His feet dragged over the dirt floor, trailing shreds of decaying gauze. Slowly, he raised his arms, making a terrifying cracking sound.

Scrape. Scrape.

My throat tightened in terror. My entire body began to tremble.

I backed away from the mummy case. Sari stood frozen with her hands pressed against her cheeks. I grabbed her arm and pulled her back with me. "Sari—get back! Get back!" I whispered.

She stared in terror at the approaching mummy. I couldn't tell if she heard me or not.

I tugged her back further.

Our backs hit the chamber wall.

The mummy scraped closer. Closer. Staring at us through its vacant, blackened eye sockets, he reached for us with his yellowed, tar-encrusted hands.

Sari let out a shrill shriek.

"Run!" I screamed. "Sari—run!"

But our backs were pressed against the wall. The mummy blocked our path to the doorway.

Moving stiffly, awkwardly, the ancient corpse dragged itself closer.

"This is all my fault!" I declared in a trembling voice. "I said the words five times. I brought him back to life!"

"Wh-what can we do?" Sari cried in a hushed whisper.

I didn't have an answer. "Uncle Ben!" I shrieked desperately. "Uncle Ben—help us!"

But the mummy case remained silent. Even my frantic screams could not awaken my uncle.

Sari and I edged along the chamber wall, our eyes locked on the approaching mummy. Its bandaged feet scraped over the floor, sending up dark clouds of dust as it moved heavily towards us.

A sour smell rose over the room. The smell of a four-thousand-year-old corpse coming to life.

I pressed my back against the cold stone of the chamber wall, my mind racing. The mummy stopped at the mummy case, turned stiffly, and continued lurching towards us.

"Hey—!" I cried out as an idea burst into my mind.

My little mummy hand. The Summoner.

Why hadn't I thought of it before? It had saved us last summer by raising a group of ancient mummies from the dead.

Could it also summon them to stop? Could it make them die again?

If I raised the little mummy hand up to Prince Khor-Ru, would it stop him long enough for Sari and me to escape?

He was only seconds away from grabbing us.

It was worth a try.

I reached into my back jeans pocket for the mummy hand.

It was gone.

"No!" I uttered a surprised cry and frantically grabbed at my other pockets.

No mummy hand.

"Gabe—what's wrong?" Sari demanded.

"The mummy hand—it's gone!" I told her, my voice choked with panic.

Scrape. Scrape.

The foul odour grew stronger as the ancient mummy dragged nearer.

I was desperate to find my mummy hand. But I knew there was no time to think about it now.

"We've got to make a run for it," I told Sari. "The mummy is slow and stiff. If we can get past him . . ."

"But what about Daddy?" she cried. "We can't just leave him here."

"We have to," I told her. "We'll get help. We'll come back for him."

The mummy made a brittle crackling sound as

it stepped forward. The sound of an ancient bone breaking.

But it continued towards us, moving stiffly but steadily, its arms outstretched.

"Sari—run—*now*!" I screamed.

I gave her a hard shove to get her going.

The room blurred as I forced myself to move.

The mummy made another loud, cracking sound. It leaned its body forward, and reached out as we dodged around it.

I tried to duck under the mummy's outstretched hand. But I felt the scrape of its ancient fingers against the back of my neck—cold fingers, hard as a statue.

I knew it was a touch I would never forget.

My neck tingled. I lowered my head from his grasp—and plunged forward.

Sari let out low sobs as she ran. My heart raced as I hurried to catch up to her. I forced myself to run, but my legs felt so heavy, as if they were made of solid stone.

We were nearly to the doorway when we saw a flickering light.

Sari and I both cried out and skidded to a stop as a beam of light swept into the room. Behind the light, a figure stepped into the doorway.

Shielding my eyes from the sudden brightness, I squinted hard, eager to see who it was.

"Nila!" I cried as she raised the torch beam to the ceiling. "Nila—help us!" I choked out.

"He's come alive!" Sari shouted to her. "Nila—he's come alive!" She pointed back towards the mummy.

"Help us!" I screamed.

Nila's green eyes widened in surprise. "What can I do?" she asked. And then her expression changed quickly to anger. "What can I do about you two kids? You shouldn't be here. You're going to ruin everything!"

"Huh?" I cried out in surprise.

Nila stepped into the room. She raised her right hand.

In the dim light, I struggled to make out what she was holding up.

My little mummy hand!

She raised it towards the mummy. "Come to me, my brother!" Nila called.

"How did you get my mummy hand? What are you doing?" I demanded.

Nila ignored my questions. She held the torch in one hand. She gripped the little hand in the other, holding it up towards the approaching mummy.

"Come here, my brother!" she called, waving the hand, summoning the mummy. "It is I, Princess Nila!"

Its legs cracking, its brittle bones breaking inside the gauze wrappings, the mummy obediently dragged itself forward.

"Nila—stop it! What are you *doing*?" Sari shrieked.

But Nila continued to ignore us. "It is I, your sister!" she called to the mummy. A triumphant smile crossed her pretty face. Her green eyes sparkled like flashing emeralds in the darting light.

"I have waited so long for this day," Nila told

the mummy. "I have waited so many centuries, my brother, hoping that someday someone would uncover your tomb and we could be reunited."

Nila's face glowed with excitement. The little mummy hand trembled in her hand. "I have brought you back to life, my brother!" she called to the mummy. "I have waited for centuries. But it will be worth it. You and I will share all this treasure. And with our powers, we shall rule Egypt together—as we did four thousand years ago!"

She lowered her eyes to me. "Thank you, Gabe!" she cried. "Thank you for The Summoner! As soon as I saw it, I knew I had to have it. I knew it could bring my brother back to me! The ancient words weren't enough. I needed The Summoner, too!"

"Give it back!" I demanded, reaching out for it. "It's mine, Nila. Give it back."

A cruel laugh escaped her throat. "You won't be needing it, Gabe," she said softly.

She waved her hand at the mummy. "Destroy them, my brother!" she ordered. "Destroy them now! There can be no witnesses!"

"Nooo!" Sari shrieked. She and I both dived to the doorway. But Nila moved quickly to block our path.

I shoved my shoulder against her, trying to push her away like an American footballer. But

Nila held her ground with surprising strength.

"Nila—let us go!" Sari demanded, breathing hard.

Nila smiled and shook her head. "No witnesses," she murmured.

"Nila—we just want to get Daddy out of here. You can do what you want!" Sari insisted desperately.

Nila ignored her and raised her eyes to the mummy. "Destroy them both!" she called. "They cannot leave this tomb alive!"

Sari and I spun around to see the mummy lumbering towards us. Its blackened skull glowed in the dim light. It trailed long strips of yellowed gauze across the dirt floor as it dragged itself closer.

Closer.

I turned back to the door. Nila blocked the way. My eyes darted frantically around the chamber.

No way to escape.

No escape.

The mummy lurched towards Sari and me.

And reached out its cold, cold hands to obey Nila's cruel command.

Sari and I darted towards the door. But Nila blocked our escape.

Its vacant eyes gazing blindly at us, its jaw frozen in a hideous skeletal grin, the mummy hurtled towards us.

Raised its arms stiffly.

Stretched out its hand.

Dived at us with a final, desperate lurch.

And to my shock, reached past Sari and me— and wrapped its tarred hands around Nila's throat.

Her mouth opened in a choked cry of protest.

The mummy tilted back its head as it gripped her. Its tarred lips moved, and a dry cough cut through the air. And then the whispered words, dry as death, escaped the mummy's throat:

"Let me . . . rest in peace!"

Nila uttered a choked cry.

The mummy tightened its fierce grip on her throat.

I spun around and grabbed its arm. "Let her go!" I screamed.

A dry wheeze erupted from the blackened skull. Its hands tightened around Nila, bending her back, bending her towards the floor.

Nila's eyes shut in defeat. Her hands flew up helplessly. The torch and the mummy hand fell to the floor.

I grabbed my little mummy hand and shoved it into my jeans pocket. "Let go! Let go! Let go!" I shrieked. I leaped on to the mummy's back and tried to pull its hands from Nila's throat.

It let out a defiant roar, a harsh whisper of anger.

Then it heaved itself up straight and struggled to toss me off its shoulders.

I gasped, startled by the mummy's surprising strength.

As I started to slide off the mummy's bandaged back, I reached out my hand, grabbing desperately, grabbing air, trying not to fall.

My hand grabbed on to Nila's amber pendant.

"Hey—!" I cried out as the mummy gave a hard toss.

I tumbled off.

The pendant tore off its chain. It fell from my hand, crashed to the floor—and shattered.

"Noooooooooo!" Nila's horrified wail shook the walls.

The mummy froze.

Nila spun out of the mummy's grasp. Backed away. Her eyes wide with terror. "My life! My *life!*" she shrieked.

She bent and struggled to pick up shards of amber from the floor. But the pendant had shattered into a hundred tiny pieces.

"My life!" Nila wailed, staring at the smooth pieces in her palm. She raised her eyes to Sari and me. "I lived inside the pendant!" she cried. "At night, I crept inside. It kept me alive for over four thousand years! And now . . . now . . . ohhhhh . . ."

As her voice trailed off, Nila began to shrink. Her head, her arms, her entire body grew tinier . . . tinier . . . until she disappeared into her clothes.

And a few seconds later, as Sari and I gaped down in horror and shock, a black scarab crawled out from under the sweatshirt and jeans. The scarab moved unsteadily at first. Then it quickly scuttled away over the dirt floor, disappearing into the darkness.

"That—that beetle—" Sari stammered. "Is it Nila?"

I nodded. "I suppose so," I said, staring down at Nila's crumpled clothes.

"Do you think she was really an ancient Egyptian princess? Prince Khor-Ru's sister?" Sari murmured.

"It's all so weird," I replied. I was thinking

hard, trying to piece it all together, trying to make sense of what Nila had said.

"She must have returned to her scarab form every night," I told Sari, thinking out loud. "She crawled into the amber and slept inside it. It kept her alive—until . . ."

"Until you smashed the amber pendant," Sari whispered.

"Yes." I nodded. "It was an accident—" I started.

But I choked on my words as I felt a cold hand close on my shoulder.

And knew that the mummy had grabbed me from behind.

The hand rested on my shoulder. The cold seeped through my T-shirt. "Let go!" I screamed.

I spun around—and my heart skipped a beat. "Uncle Ben!" I cried.

"Daddy!" Sari leaped forward and threw her arms around him. "Daddy—you're okay!"

He pulled his hand off my shoulder and rubbed the back of his head. He blinked his eyes uncertainly and shook his head, still a little dazed.

Behind him, I saw the mummy standing hunched over, frozen. Lifeless once again.

"Whew. I'm still groggy," Uncle Ben said, sweeping a hand back through his thick, black hair. "What a close call."

"It's all my fault," I admitted. "I repeated the words five times, Uncle Ben. I didn't mean to bring the mummy back to life, but—"

A smile crossed my uncle's face. He lowered his arm around my shoulders. "You didn't do it,

115

Gabe," he said softly. "Nila got there first."

He sighed. "I didn't believe in the power of the chant," he said softly. "But I do now. Nila stole your mummy hand and chanted the ancient words. She used The Summoner to bring the mummy to life. Dr Fielding and I were both suspicious of her."

"You were?" I cried, surprised. "But I thought—"

"I became suspicious of Nila at dinner," Uncle Ben explained. "Remember? She asked me what were the *six* ancient words to bring the dead to life? Well, I had never revealed that there were six. So I wondered how Nila knew there were six words."

Uncle Ben put an arm around Sari's shoulders, too, and led us to the wall. Then he leaned his back against the wall, rubbing the back of his head.

"That's why I hurried to the communications tent straight after dinner," Uncle Ben continued. "I phoned the Cairo *Sun*. They had never heard of Nila at the newspaper. So I knew she was a fake."

"But we saw Dr Fielding pull you from the tent," Sari broke in. "We saw him force you into the pyramid, and—"

Uncle Ben chuckled. "You two aren't very good spies," he scolded. "Dr Fielding didn't force me to do anything. He had spotted Nila sneaking into the pyramid. So he found me at the communications tent. And the two of us hurried to the pyramid to see what Nila was up to.

"We got there too late," Uncle Ben continued. "She had already brought the mummy to life. Dr Fielding and I tried to stop her. She hit me over the head with her torch. She dragged me to the mummy case. I guess she stuffed me inside."

He rubbed his head. "That's all I remember. Until now. Until I awoke and saw Nila turn into a scarab."

"We saw Dr Fielding hurry out of the pyramid," Sari reported. "He walked right past me. He had the weirdest look on his face, and—"

She stopped and her mouth dropped open. We all heard the sounds at the same time.

The scraping of feet on the floor outside the burial chamber.

My heart jumped to my throat. I grabbed Uncle Ben's arm.

The footsteps dragged closer.

More mummies.

More mummies brought to life, staggering towards the prince's tomb.

I reached into my jeans pocket for my little mummy hand. Pressing my back against the wall, I raised my eyes to the chamber doorway—and waited.

Waited for the mummies to appear.

But to my surprise, Dr Fielding burst into the room, followed by four dark-uniformed police officers, hands at their gun holsters.

"Ben—are you okay?" Dr Fielding called to my uncle. "Where is the young woman?"

"She . . . escaped," Uncle Ben told him.

How could he explain that she had turned into a bug?

The police explored the chamber warily. Their eyes came to rest on the mummy, frozen in place near the doorway.

"I'm so glad you're okay, Ben," Dr Fielding said, placing a hand warmly on Uncle Ben's shoulder. Then he turned to Sari. "I'm afraid I owe you an apology, Sari," he said, frowning.

"When I ran out of here, I must have been in shock. I remember seeing you outside the pyramid. But I don't remember saying anything to you."

"That's okay," Sari replied quietly.

"I'm really sorry if I frightened you," Dr Fielding told her. "Your dad had been knocked unconscious by that crazy young woman. And all I could think about was calling the police as fast as possible."

"Well, the excitement is over," Uncle Ben said, smiling. "Let's all get out of here."

We started towards the doorway, but a police officer interrupted. "Could I just ask one question?" he asked, staring at the upright mummy in the centre of the floor. "Did that mummy walk?"

"Of course not!" Uncle Ben replied quickly, a grin spreading over his face. "If it could walk, what would it be doing in *this* dump?"

Well, once again, I turned out to be the hero of the day. And, of course, later in the tent, I wasted no time in bragging about my courage to Sari.

Sari had no choice. She had to sit there and take it. After all, *I* was the one who had stopped the mummy and turned Nila back into a beetle by smashing her pendant.

"At least you're not too conceited!" Sari shot back, rolling her eyes.

119

Lame. Really lame.

"Well, that scarab crawled away and disappeared," she said. An evil smile crossed Sari's lips. "I bet that bug is waiting for you, Gabe. I bet it's waiting for you in your camp bed, waiting to bite you."

I laughed. "Sari, you'd say anything to try to scare me. You just can't stand the idea that *I'm* the hero!"

"You're right," she replied dryly. "I *can't* stand the idea. Good night, Gabe."

A few minutes later, I was in my pyjamas and ready for bed. What a night! What an amazing night!

As I slid into the bed and pulled up the covers, I knew it was a night I would never forget.

"Ouch!"

The Scarecrow Walks
at Midnight

"Hey, Jodie—wait up!"

I turned and squinted into the bright sunlight. My brother, Mark, was still on the concrete train platform. The train had clattered off. I could see it snaking its way through the low, green meadows in the distance.

I turned to Stanley. Stanley is the hired man on my grandparents' farm. He stood beside me, carrying both suitcases. "Look in the dictionary for the word 'slowpoke'," I said, "and you'll see Mark's picture."

Stanley smiled at me. "I like the dictionary, Jodie," he said. "Sometimes I read it for hours."

"Hey, Mark—get a move on!" I cried. But he was taking his time, walking slowly, in a daze as usual.

I tossed my blonde hair behind my shoulders and turned back to Stanley. Mark and I hadn't visited the farm for a year. But Stanley still looked the same.

He's so skinny. "Like a noodle," my grandma always says. His denim overalls always look five sizes too big on him.

Stanley is about forty or forty-five, I think. He wears his dark hair in a crewcut, shaved close to his head. His ears are huge. They stick way out and are always bright red. And he has big, round, brown eyes that remind me of puppy eyes.

Stanley isn't very smart. Grandpa Kurt always says that Stanley isn't working with a full one hundred watts.

But Mark and I really like him. He has a quiet sense of humour. And he is kind and gentle and friendly, and always has lots of amazing things to show us whenever we visit the farm.

"You look nice, Jodie," Stanley said, his cheeks turning as red as his ears. "How old are you now?"

"Twelve," I told him. "And Mark is eleven."

He thought about it. "That makes twenty-three," he joked.

We both laughed. You never know *what* Stanley is going to say!

"I think I stepped in something gross," Mark complained, catching up with us.

I *always* know what Mark is going to say. My brother only knows three words—*cool, weird*, and *gross*. Really. That's his whole vocabulary.

As a joke, I gave him a dictionary for his last birthday. "You're *weird*," Mark said when I handed it to him. "What a *gross* gift."

He scraped his white trainers on the ground as we followed Stanley to the beat-up, red pick-up truck. "Carry my backpack for me," Mark said, trying to shove the bulging backpack at me.

"No way," I told him. "Carry it yourself."

The backpack contained his Walkman, about thirty tapes, comic books, his Game Boy, and at least fifty game cartridges. I knew he planned to spend the whole month lying on the hammock on the screened-in back porch of the farmhouse, listening to music and playing video games.

Well . . . no way!

Mum and Dad said it was *my* job to make sure Mark got outside and enjoyed the farm. We were so cooped up in the city all year. That's why they sent us to visit Grandpa Kurt and Grandma Miriam for a month each summer—to enjoy the great outdoors.

We stopped beside the truck while Stanley searched his overall pockets for the key. "It's going to get pretty hot today," Stanley said, "unless it cools down."

A typical Stanley weather report.

I gazed out at the wide, grassy field beyond the small railway station car park. Thousands of tiny white puffballs floated up against the clear blue sky.

125

It was so beautiful!

Naturally, I sneezed.

I love visiting my grandparents' farm. My only problem is, I'm allergic to just about everything on it.

So Mum packs several bottles of my allergy medicine for me—and lots of tissues.

"*Gesundheit,*" Stanley said. He tossed our two suitcases in the back of the pick-up. Mark slid his backpack in, too. "Can I ride in the back?" he asked.

He loves to lie flat in the back, staring up at the sky, and bumping up and down really hard.

Stanley is a terrible driver. He can't seem to concentrate on steering and driving at the right speed at the same time. So there are always lots of quick turns and heavy bumps.

Mark lifted himself into the back of the pick-up and stretched out next to the suitcases. I climbed beside Stanley in the front.

A short while later, we were bouncing along the narrow, twisting road that led to the farm. I stared out of the dusty window at the passing meadows and farmhouses. Everything looked so green and alive.

Stanley drove with both hands wrapped tightly around the top of the steering wheel. He sat forward stiffly, leaning over the wheel, staring straight ahead through the windscreen without blinking.

"Mr Mortimer doesn't farm his place any more," he said, lifting one hand from the wheel to point to a big, white farmhouse on top of a sloping, green hill.

"Why not?" I asked.

"Because he died," Stanley replied solemnly.

See what I mean? You never know what Stanley is going to say.

We bounced over a deep rut in the road. I was sure Mark was having a great time in the back.

The road leads through the small town, so small that it doesn't even have a name. The farmers have always called it Town.

It has a feed store, a combined petrol station and grocery store, a white-steepled church, a hardware store, and a post box.

There were two trucks parked in front of the feed store. I didn't see anyone as we barrelled past.

My grandparents' farm is about two miles from town. I recognized the cornfields as we approached.

"The corn is so high already!" I exclaimed, staring through the bouncing window. "Have you eaten any yet?"

"Just at dinner," Stanley replied.

Suddenly, he slowed the truck and turned his eyes to me. "The scarecrow walks at midnight," he uttered in a low voice.

"Huh?" I wasn't sure I'd heard correctly.

"The scarecrow walks at midnight," he repeated, training his big puppy eyes on me. "I read it in the book."

I didn't know what to say, so I laughed. I thought maybe he was making a joke.

Days later, I realized it was no joke.

Watching the farm spread out in front of us filled me with happiness. It's not a big farm or a fancy farm, but I like everything about it.

I like the barn with its sweet smells. I like the low mooing sounds of the cows way off in the far pasture. I like to watch the tall stalks of corn, all swaying together in the wind.

Corny, huh?

I also like the scary ghost stories Grandpa Kurt tells us at night in front of the fireplace.

And I have to include Grandma Miriam's chocolate chip pancakes. They're so good, I sometimes dream about them back home in the city.

I also like the happy expressions on my grandparents' faces when we come rushing up to greet them.

Of course I was the first one out of the truck. Mark was as slow as usual. I went running up to the screen porch at the back of their big, old farmhouse. I couldn't *wait* to see my grand-parents.

Grandma Miriam came waddling out, her arms outstretched. The screen door slammed behind her. But then I saw Grandpa Kurt push it open and he hurried out, too.

His limp was worse, I noticed right away. He leaned heavily on a white stick. He'd never needed one before.

I didn't have time to think about it as Mark and I were smothered in hugs. "So good to see you! It's been so long, so long!" Grandma Miriam cried happily.

There were the usual comments about how much taller we were and how grown up we looked.

"Jodie, where'd you get that blonde hair? There aren't any blondes in *my* family," Grandpa Kurt would say, shaking his mane of white hair. "You must get that from your father's side.

"No, I know. I bet you got it from a store," he said, grinning. It was his little joke. He greeted me with it every summer. And his blue eyes would sparkle excitedly.

"You're right. It's a wig," I told him, laughing. He gave my long blonde hair a playful tug.

"Have you got cable yet?" Mark asked, dragging his backpack along the ground.

"Cable TV?" Grandpa Kurt stared hard at

Mark. "Not yet. But we still get three channels. How many more do we need?"

Mark rolled his eyes. "No MTV," he groaned.

Stanley made his way past us, carrying our suitcases into the house.

"Let's go in. I'll bet you're starving," Grandma Miriam said. "I made soup and sandwiches. We'll have chicken and corn tonight. The corn is very sweet this year. I know how you two love it."

I watched my grandparents as they led the way to the house. They both looked older to me. They moved more slowly than I remembered. Grandpa Kurt's limp was definitely worse. They both seemed tired.

Grandma Miriam is short and chubby. She has a round face surrounded by curly red hair. Bright red. There's no way to describe the colour. I don't know what she uses to dye it that colour. I've never seen it on anyone else!

She wears square-shaped glasses that give her a really old-fashioned look. She likes big, roomy dresses. I don't think I've ever seen her in jeans or trousers.

Grandpa Kurt is tall and broad-shouldered. Mum says he was really handsome when he was young. "Like a movie star," she always tells me.

Now he has wavy, white hair, still very thick, that he wets and slicks down flat on his head. He has sparkling blue eyes that always make me smile. And white stubble over his slender face. Grandpa Kurt doesn't like to shave.

Today he was wearing a long-sleeved, red-and-green-plaid shirt, buttoned to the collar despite the hot day, and baggy jeans, stained at one knee, held up by white braces.

Lunch was fun. We sat around the long kitchen table. Sunlight poured in through the big window. I could see the barn at the back and the cornfields stretching behind it.

Mark and I told all our news—about school, about my basketball team going to the championships, about our new car, about Dad growing a moustache.

For some reason, Stanley thought that was very funny. He was laughing so hard, he choked on his split-pea soup. And Grandpa Kurt had to reach over and slap him on the back.

It's hard to know what will crack Stanley up. As Mark would say, Stanley is definitely *weird*.

All through lunch, I kept staring at my grandparents. I couldn't get over how much they had changed in one year. They seemed so much quieter, so much slower.

That's what it means to get older, I told myself.

"Stanley will have to show you his scarecrows," Grandma Miriam said, passing the bowl of crisps. "Won't you, Stanley?"

Grandpa Kurt cleared his throat loudly. I had

the feeling he was telling Grandma Miriam to change the subject or something.

"I made them," Stanley said, grinning proudly. He turned his big eyes on me. "The book—it told me how."

"Are you still taking guitar lessons?" Grandpa Kurt asked Mark.

I could see that, for some reason, Grandpa Kurt didn't want to talk about Stanley's scarecrows.

"Yeah," Mark answered with a mouthful of crisps. "But I sold my acoustic. I switched to electric."

"You mean you have to plug it in?" Stanley asked. He started to giggle, as if he had just cracked a funny joke.

"What a shame you didn't bring your guitar," Grandma Miriam said to Mark.

"No, it isn't," I teased. "The cows would start giving sour milk!"

"Shut up, Jodie!" Mark snapped. He has no sense of humour.

"They already *do* give sour milk," Grandpa Kurt muttered, lowering his eyes.

"Bad luck. When cows give sour milk, it means bad luck," Stanley declared, his eyes widening, his expression suddenly fearful.

"It's okay, Stanley," Grandma Miriam assured him quickly, placing a hand gently on his shoulder. "Grandpa Kurt was only teasing."

"If you kids are finished, why not go with Stanley," Grandpa Kurt said. "He'll give you a tour of the farm. You always enjoy that." He sighed. "I'd go along, but my leg—it's been acting up again."

Grandma Miriam started to clear the dishes. Mark and I followed Stanley out of the back door. The grass in the back yard had recently been mown. The air was heavy with its sweet smell.

I saw a hummingbird fluttering over the flower garden beside the house. I pointed it out to Mark, but by the time he turned, it had hummed away.

At the back of the long, green yard stood the old barn. Its white walls were badly stained and peeling. It really needed a paint job. The doors were open, and I could see square bales of straw inside.

Far to the right of the barn, almost to the cornfields, stood the small guest house where Stanley lived with his teenage son, Sticks.

"Stanley—where's Sticks?" I asked. "Why wasn't he at lunch?"

"Went to town," Stanley answered quietly. "Went to town, riding on a pony."

Mark and I exchanged glances. We never can figure Stanley out.

Poking up from the cornfield stood several dark figures, the scarecrows Grandma Miriam had started to talk about. I stared out at them, shielding my eyes from the sun with one hand.

"So many scarecrows!" I exclaimed. "Stanley, last summer there was only one. Why are there so many now?"

He didn't reply. He didn't seem to hear me. He had a black baseball cap pulled down low over his forehead. He was taking long strides, leaning forward with that stork-like walk of his, his hands shoved into the pockets of his baggy denim overalls.

"We've seen the farm a hundred times," Mark complained, whispering to me. "Why do we have to take the grand tour again?"

"Mark—chill out," I told him. "We *always* take a tour of the farm. It's a tradition."

Mark grumbled to himself. He really is lazy. He never wants to do anything.

Stanley led the way past the barn into the cornfields. The stalks were way over my head. Their golden tassels gleamed in the bright sunlight.

Stanley reached up and pulled an ear off the stalk. "Let's see if it's ready," he said, grinning at Mark and me.

He held the ear in his left hand and started to strip it with his right.

After a few seconds, he pulled the husk away, revealing the ear of corn inside.

I stared at it—and let out a horrified cry.

"Ohhhh—it's *disgusting*!" I shrieked.

"Gross!" I heard Mark groan.

The corn was a disgusting brown colour. And it was *moving* on the cob. Wriggling. Squirming.

Stanley raised the corn to his face to examine it. And I realized it was covered with worms. Hundreds of wriggling, brown worms.

"No!" Stanley cried in horror. He let the ear of corn drop to the ground at his feet. "That's bad luck! The book says so. That's very bad luck!"

I stared down at the ear of corn. The worms were wriggling off the cob, on to the dirt.

"It's okay, Stanley," I told him. "I only screamed because I was surprised. This happens sometimes. Sometimes worms get into the corn. Grandpa told me."

"No. It's bad," Stanley insisted in a trembling voice. His red ears were aflame. His big eyes revealed his fear. "The book—it says so."

"What book?" Mark demanded. He kicked the

136

wormy ear of corn away with the toe of his trainer.

"My book," Stanley replied mysteriously. "My superstition book."

Uh-oh, I thought. Stanley shouldn't have a book about superstitions. He was already the most superstitious person in the world—even without a book!

"You've been reading a book about superstitions?" Mark asked him, watching the brown worms crawl over the soft dirt.

"Yes." Stanley nodded his head enthusiastically. "It's a good book. It tells me everything. And it's all true. All of it!"

He pulled off his cap and scratched his stubby hair. "I've got to check the book. I've got to see what to do about the corn. The bad corn."

He was getting pretty worked up. It was making me feel a little scared. I've known Stanley my whole life. I think he's worked for Grandpa Kurt for more than twenty years. He's always been strange. But I've never seen him get so upset about something as unimportant as a bad ear of corn.

"Show us the scarecrows," I said, trying to get his mind off the corn.

"Yeah. Let's see them," Mark joined in.

"Okay. The scarecrows." Stanley nodded. Then he turned, still thinking hard, and began leading the way through the tall rows of cornstalks.

The stalks creaked and groaned as we passed by them. It was an eerie sound.

Suddenly, a shadow fell over me. One of the dark scarecrows rose up in front of us. It wore a tattered black coat, stuffed with straw. Its arms stretched stiffly out at its sides.

The scarecrow was tall, towering over my head. Tall enough to stand over the high cornstalks.

Its head was a faded sack, filled with straw. Evil black eyes and a menacing frown had been painted on thickly in black paint. A battered old-fashioned hat rested on its head.

"You made these?" I asked Stanley. I could see several other scarecrows poking up from the corn. They all stood in the same stiff position. They all had the same menacing frown.

He stared up at the scarecrow's face. "I made them," he said in a low voice. "The book showed me how."

"They're pretty scary-looking," Mark said, standing close beside me. He grabbed the scarecrow's straw hand and shook it. "What's up?" Mark asked it.

"The scarecrow walks at midnight," Stanley said, repeating the phrase he had used at the train station.

Mark was trying to slap the scarecrow a high-five.

"What does that *mean*?" I asked Stanley.

"The book told me how," Stanley replied, keeping his eyes on the dark-painted face on the sack. "The book told me how to make them walk."

"Huh? You mean you make the scarecrows *walk*?" I asked, very confused.

Stanley's dark eyes locked on mine. Once again, he got that very solemn expression on his face. "I know how to do it. The book has all the words."

I stared back at him, totally confused. I didn't know what to say.

"I made them walk, Jodie," Stanley continued in a voice just above a whisper. "I made them walk last week. And now I'm the boss."

"Huh? The boss of the s-scarecrows?" I stammered. "Do you mean—"

I stopped when, out of the corner of my eye, I saw the scarecrow's arm move.

The straw crinkled as the arm slid up.

Then I felt rough straw brush against my face—as the dry scarecrow arm moved to my throat.

The prickly straw, poking out of the sleeve of the black coat, scraped against my neck.

I let out a shrill scream.

"It's *alive*!" I cried in panic, diving to the ground, scrambling away on all fours.

I turned back to see Mark and Stanley calmly watching me.

Hadn't they seen the scarecrow try to choke me?

Then Stanley's son, Sticks, stepped out from behind the scarecrow, a gleeful grin on his face.

"Sticks—! You creep!" I cried angrily. I knew at once that he had moved the scarecrow's arm.

"You city kids sure scare easy," Sticks said, his grin growing wider. He reached down to help me to my feet. "You really thought the scarecrow moved, didn't you, Jodie!" he said accusingly.

"I can make the scarecrows move," Stanley said, pulling the cap down lower on his forehead.

140

"I can make them walk. I did it. It's all in the book."

Sticks's smile faded. The light seemed to dim from his dark eyes. "Yeah, sure, Dad," he murmured.

Sticks is sixteen. He is tall and lanky. He has long, skinny arms and legs. That's how he got the nickname Sticks.

He tries to look tough. He has long black hair down past his collar, which he seldom washes. He wears tight muscle shirts and dirty jeans, ripped at the knees. He sneers a lot, and his dark eyes always seem to be laughing at you.

He calls Mark and me "the city kids". He always says it with a sneer. And he's always playing stupid jokes on us. I think he's a bit jealous of Mark and me. I don't think it's been easy for Sticks to grow up on the farm, living in the little guest house with his dad.

I mean, Stanley is more like a kid than a father.

"I saw you back there," Mark told Sticks.

"Well, thanks for warning me!" I snapped at Mark. I turned back angrily to Sticks. "I see you haven't changed at all."

"Great to see you, too, Jodie," he replied sarcastically. "The city kids are back for another month with the hicks!"

"Sticks—what's your problem?" I shot back.

"Be nice," Stanley muttered. "The corn has ears, you know."

We all stared at Stanley. Had he just made a joke? It was hard to tell with him.

Stanley's face remained serious. His big eyes stared out at me through the shade of his cap. "The corn has ears," he repeated. "There are spirits in the field."

Sticks shook his head unhappily. "Dad, you spend too much time with that superstition book," he muttered.

"The book is all true," Stanley replied. "It's all true."

Sticks kicked at the dirt. He raised his eyes to me. His expression seemed very sad. "Things are different here," he murmured.

"Huh?" I didn't understand. "What do you mean?"

Sticks turned to his father. Stanley was staring back at him, his eyes narrowed.

Sticks shrugged and didn't reply. He grabbed Mark's arm and squeezed it. "You're as flabby as ever," he told Mark. "Want to throw a football around this afternoon?"

"It's a bit hot," Mark replied. He wiped the sweat off his forehead with the back of his hand.

Sticks sneered at him. "Still a wimp, huh?"

"No way!" Mark protested. "I just said it was hot, that's all."

"Hey—you've got something on your back," Sticks told Mark. "Turn around."

Mark obediently turned around.

Sticks quickly bent down, picked up the wormy corn-cob, and stuffed it down the back of Mark's T-shirt.

I had to laugh as I watched my brother run screaming all the way back to the farmhouse.

Dinner was quiet. Grandma Miriam's fried chicken was as tasty as ever. And she was right about the corn. It was very sweet. Mark and I each ate two ears, dripping with butter.

I enjoyed the dinner. But it upset me that both of my grandparents seemed so changed. Grandpa Kurt used to talk non-stop. He always had dozens of funny stories about the farmers in the area. And he always had new jokes to tell.

Tonight he barely said a word.

Grandma Miriam kept urging Mark and me to eat more. And she kept asking us how we liked everything. But she, too, seemed quieter.

They both seemed tense. Uncomfortable.

They both kept glancing down the table at Stanley, who was eating with both hands, butter dripping down his chin.

Sticks sat glumly across from his father. He seemed even more unfriendly than usual.

143

Stanley was the only cheerful person at the table. He chewed his chicken enthusiastically and asked for a third helping of mashed potatoes.

"Is everything okay, Stanley?" Grandma Miriam kept asking, biting her bottom lip. "Everything okay?"

Stanley burped and smiled. "Not bad," was his reply.

Why do things seem so different? I wondered. Is it just because Grandma and Grandpa are getting old?

After dinner, we sat around the big, comfortable living room. Grandpa Kurt rocked gently back and forth in the antique wooden rocking chair by the fireplace.

It was too hot to build a fire. But as he rocked, he stared into the dark fireplace, a thoughtful expression on his white-stubbled face.

Grandma Miriam sat in her favourite chair, a big green overstuffed armchair across from Grandpa Kurt. She had an unopened gardening magazine in her lap.

Sticks, who had barely said two words the whole evening, disappeared. Stanley leaned against the wall, poking his teeth with a toothpick.

Mark sank down into the long, green couch. I sat down at the other end of it and stared across the room.

144

"Yuck. That stuffed bear still gives me the creeps!" I exclaimed.

At the far end of the room, an enormous stuffed brown bear—about eight feet tall—stood straight up on its hind legs. Grandpa Kurt had shot it many years ago on a hunting trip. The bear's huge paws were extended, as if ready to pounce.

"That was a killer bear," Grandpa Kurt remembered, rocking slowly, his eyes on the angry-looking beast. "He mauled two hunters before I shot him. I saved their lives."

I shuddered and turned away from the bear. I really hated it. I don't know why Grandma Miriam let Grandpa Kurt keep it in the living room!

"How about a scary story?" I asked Grandpa Kurt.

He stared back at me, his blue eyes suddenly lifeless and dull.

"Yeah. We've been looking forward to your stories," Mark chimed in. "Tell us the one about the headless boy in the closet."

"No. Tell a new one," I insisted eagerly.

Grandpa Kurt rubbed his chin slowly. His eyes went to Stanley across the room. Then he cleared his throat nervously.

"I'm a bit tired, kids," he said softly. "Think I'll just go to bed."

"But—no story?" I protested.

145

He stared back at me with those dull eyes. "I don't really know any stories," he murmured. He slowly climbed to his feet and headed towards his room.

What is going on here? I asked myself. *What is wrong?*

Upstairs in my bedroom later that night, I changed into a long nightshirt. The bedroom window was open, and a soft breeze invaded the room.

I stared out of the open window. A broad apple tree cast its shadow over the lawn.

Where the grass ended, the cornfields stretched out under the glow of the full moon. The pale moonlight made the tall stalks shimmer like gold. The stalks cast long blue shadows over the field.

Across the wide field, the scarecrows poked up stiffly like dark-uniformed soldiers. Their coat sleeves ruffled in the light breeze. Their pale sack faces seemed to stare back at me.

I felt a cold chill run down my back.

So many scarecrows. At least a dozen of them, standing in straight rows. Like an army ready to march.

"The scarecrow walks at midnight."

That's what Stanley had said in that low, frightening tone I had never heard him use before.

I glanced at the clock on the bed table. Just past ten o'clock.

I'll be asleep by the time they walk, I thought. A crazy thought.

I sneezed. It seems I'm allergic to the farm air both day *and* night!

I stared at the long shadows cast by the scarecrows. A gust of wind bent the stalks, making the shadows roll forward like a dark ocean wave.

And then I saw the scarecrows start to twitch.

"Mark!" I screamed. "Mark—come here! Hurry!"

Under the light of the full moon, I stared in horror as the dark scarecrows started to move.

Their arms jerked. Their sack heads lurched forward.

All of them. In unison.

All of the scarecrows were jerking, twitching, straining—as if struggling to pull free of their stakes.

"Mark—hurry!" I screamed.

I heard footsteps clomping rapidly down the hall. Mark burst breathlessly into my room. "Jodie—what *is* it?" he cried.

I motioned frantically for him to come to the window. As he stepped beside me, I pointed to the cornfields. "Look—the scarecrows."

He gripped the window-sill and leaned out of the window.

Over his shoulder, I could see the scarecrows twitch in unison. A cold shudder made me wrap my arms around myself.

149

"It's the wind," Mark said, stepping back from the window. "What's your problem, Jodie? It's just the wind blowing them around."

"You—you're wrong, Mark," I stammered, still hugging myself. "Look again."

He rolled his eyes and sighed. But he turned back and leaned out of the window. He gazed out at the field for a long time.

"Don't you see?" I demanded shrilly. "They're all moving together. Their arms, their heads—all moving together."

When Mark pulled back from the window, his blue eyes were wide and fearful. He stared at me thoughtfully and didn't say a word.

Finally, he swallowed hard and his voice came out low and frightened. "We've got to tell Grandpa Kurt," he said.

We rushed downstairs, but our grandparents had gone to bed. The bedroom door was closed. It was silent on the other side.

"Maybe we'd better wait till tomorrow morning," I whispered as Mark and I tiptoed back upstairs to our rooms. "I think we'll be safe till then."

We crept back to our rooms. I pushed the window shut and locked it. Out in the fields, the scarecrows were still twitching, still pulling at their stakes.

With a shudder, I turned away from the

150

window and plunged into the bed, pulling the old quilt up over my head.

I slept restlessly, tossing under the heavy quilt. In the morning, I jumped eagerly from bed. I ran a brush through my hair and hurried down to breakfast.

Mark was right behind me on the stairs. He was wearing the same jeans as yesterday and a red-and-black Nirvana T-shirt. He hadn't bothered to brush his hair. It stood straight up at the back.

"Pancakes!" he managed to choke out. Mark is only good for one word at a time this early in the morning.

But the word instantly cheered me up and made me forget for a moment about the creepy scarecrows.

How could I have forgotten about Grandma Miriam's amazing chocolate chip pancakes?

They are so soft, they really do melt in your mouth. And the warm chocolate mixed with the sweet maple syrup makes the most delicious breakfast I've ever eaten.

As we hurried across the living room towards the kitchen, I sniffed the air, hoping to smell that wonderful aroma of pancake batter on the stove.

But my nose was too stuffed up to smell anything.

Mark and I burst into the kitchen at the same time. Grandpa Kurt and Stanley were already at the table. A big blue pot of coffee stood steaming in front of them.

Stanley sipped his coffee. Grandpa Kurt had his face buried behind the morning newspaper. He glanced up and smiled as Mark and I entered.

Everyone said good morning to everyone.

Mark and I took our places at the table. We were so eager for the famous pancakes, we were practically rubbing our hands together the way cartoon characters do.

Imagine our shock when Grandma Miriam set down big bowls of cornflakes in front of us.

I practically burst into tears.

I glanced across the table at Mark. He was staring back at me, his face revealing his surprise—and disappointment. "Cornflakes?" he asked in a high-pitched voice.

Grandma Miriam had gone back to the sink. I turned to her. "Grandma Miriam—no pancakes?" I asked meekly.

I saw her glance at Stanley. "I've stopped making them, Jodie," she replied, her eyes still on Stanley. "Pancakes are too fattening."

"Nothing like a good bowl of cornflakes in the morning," Stanley said with a big smile. He reached for the cornflakes box in the centre of the table and filled his bowl up with a second helping.

Grandpa Kurt grunted behind his newspaper.

"Go ahead—eat them before they get soggy,"

Grandma Miriam urged from the sink.

Mark and I just stared at each other. Last summer, Grandma Miriam had made us a big stack of chocolate chip pancakes almost every morning!

What is going on here? I wondered once again.

I suddenly remembered Sticks out in the cornfields the day before, whispering to me, "Things are different here."

They sure were different. And not for the better, I decided.

My stomach grumbled. I picked up the spoon and started to eat my cornflakes. I saw Mark glumly spooning his. And then I suddenly remembered the twitching scarecrows.

"Grandpa Kurt—" I started. "Last night, Mark and I—we were looking out at the cornfields and we saw the scarecrows. They were moving. We—"

I heard Grandma Miriam utter a low gasp from behind me.

Grandpa Kurt lowered his newspaper. He narrowed his eyes at me, but didn't say a word.

"The scarecrows were moving!" Mark chimed in.

Stanley chuckled. "It was the wind," he said, his eyes on Grandpa Kurt. "It had to be the wind blowing them around."

Grandpa Kurt glared at Stanley. "You sure?" he demanded.

"Yeah. It was the wind," Stanley replied tensely.

"But they were trying to get off their poles!" I cried. "We *saw* them!"

Grandpa Kurt stared hard at Stanley.

Stanley's ears turned bright red. He lowered his eyes. "It was a breezy night," he said. "They move in the wind."

"It's going to be a sunny day," Grandma Miriam said brightly from the sink.

"But the scarecrows—" Mark insisted.

"Yep. Looks like a real pretty day," Grandpa Kurt mumbled, ignoring Mark.

He doesn't want to talk about the scarecrows, I realized.

Is it because he doesn't believe us?

Grandpa Kurt turned to Stanley. "After you take the cows to the pasture, maybe you and Jodie and Mark can do some fishing at the creek."

"Maybe," Stanley replied, studying the cornflakes box. "Maybe we could just do that."

"Sounds like fun," Mark said. Mark likes fishing. It's one of his favourite sports because you don't have to move too much.

There's a really pretty creek behind the cows' pasture at the far end of Grandpa Kurt's property. It's wooded back there, and the narrow creek trickles softly beneath the trees and is usually filled with fish.

154

Finishing my cereal, I turned to Grandma Miriam at the sink. "And what are you doing today?" I asked her. "Maybe you and I could spend some time together and—"

I stopped as she turned towards me and her hand came into view.

"Ohhhh." I let out a frightened moan when I saw her hand. It—it was made of *straw*!

"Jodie—what's the matter?" Grandma Miriam asked.

I started to point to her hand.

Then it came into sharp focus, and I saw that her hand wasn't straw—she was holding a broom.

She had gripped it by the handle and was pulling lint off the ends of the straw.

"Nothing's wrong," I told her, feeling like a total jerk. I rubbed my eyes. "I've got to take my allergy medicine," I told her. "My eyes are so watery. I keep *seeing* things!"

I was seeing scarecrows everywhere I looked!

I scolded myself for acting so crazy.

Stop thinking about scarecrows, I told myself. Stanley was right. The scarecrows had moved in the wind last night.

It was just the wind.

Stanley took us fishing later that morning. As

we started off for the creek, he seemed in a really cheerful mood.

He smiled as he swung the big picnic basket Grandma Miriam had packed for our lunch. "She put in all my favourites," Stanley said happily.

He patted the basket with childish satisfaction.

He had three bamboo fishing rods tucked under his left arm. He carried the big straw basket in his right hand. He refused to let Mark and me carry anything.

The warm air smelled sweet. The sun beamed down in a cloudless blue sky. Blades of recently cut grass stuck to my white trainers as we headed across the back yard.

The medicine had helped. My eyes were much better.

Stanley turned just past the barn and began walking quickly along its back wall. His expression turned solemn. He appeared to be concentrating hard on something.

"Hey—where are we going?" I called, hurrying to keep up with him.

He didn't seem to hear me. Taking long strides, swinging the straw picnic basket as he walked, he headed back in the direction we started from.

"Hey—wait up!" Mark called breathlessly. My

brother hates to hurry when he can take his time.

"Stanley—wait!" I cried, tugging his shirtsleeve. "We're going round in circles!"

He nodded, his expression serious under the black baseball cap. "We have to circle the barn three times," he said in a low voice.

"Huh? Why?" I demanded.

We started our second turn round the barn.

"It will bring us good luck with our fishing," Stanley replied. Then he added, "It's in the book. Everything is in the book."

I opened my mouth to tell him this was really silly. But I decided not to. He seemed so serious about that superstition book of his. I didn't want to spoil it for him.

Besides, Mark and I could do with the exercise.

A short while later, we finished circling and started walking along the dirt path that led past the cornfields to the creek. Stanley's smile returned immediately.

He really believes the superstitions in the book, I realized.

I wondered if Sticks believed them, too.

"Where's Sticks?" I asked, kicking a big clump of dirt across the path.

"Doing chores," Stanley replied. "Sticks is a good worker. A really good worker. But he'll be along soon, I bet. Sticks never likes to miss out on a fishing trip."

The sun began to feel really strong on my face and on my shoulders. I wondered if I should run back and get some sunblock.

The dark-suited scarecrows appeared to stare at me as we walked past the tall rows of cornstalks. I could swear their pale, painted faces turned to follow me as I went by.

And did one of them lift its arm to wave a straw hand at me?

I scolded myself for having such stupid thoughts, and turned my eyes away.

Stop thinking about scarecrows, Jodie! I told myself.

Forget your bad dream. Forget about the stupid scarecrows.

It's a beautiful day, and you have nothing to worry about. Try to relax and have a good time.

The path led into tall pine woods behind the cornfields. It got shady and much cooler as soon as we stepped into the woods.

"Can't we take a taxi the rest of the way?" Mark whined. A typical Mark joke. He really *would* take a taxi if there was one!

Stanley shook his head. "City kids," he muttered, grinning.

The path ended, and we continued through the trees. It smelled so piney and fresh in the woods. I saw a tiny, brown-and-white chipmunk dart into a hollow log.

In the near distance I could hear the musical trickle of the creek.

Suddenly, Stanley stopped. He bent and picked up a pine cone.

The three fishing rods fell to the ground. He didn't seem to notice. He held the pine cone close to his face, studying it.

"A pine cone on the shady side means a long winter," he said, turning the dry cone in his hand.

Mark and I bent to pick up the rods. "Is that what the book says?" Mark asked.

Stanley nodded. He set the pine cone down carefully where he found it.

"The cone is still sticky. That's a good sign," he said seriously.

Mark let out a giggle. I knew he was trying not to laugh at Stanley. But the giggle escaped somehow.

Stanley's big brown eyes filled with hurt. "It's all true, Mark," he said quietly. "It's all true."

"I—I'd like to read that book," Mark said, glancing at me.

"It's a very hard book," Stanley replied. "I have trouble with some of the words."

"I can hear the creek," I broke in, changing the subject. "Let's go. I want to catch some fish before lunchtime."

The clear water felt cold against my legs. The

smooth rocks of the creek bed were slippery under my bare feet.

All three of us had waded into the shallow creek. Mark had wanted to lie down on the grassy shore to fish. But I convinced him it was much more fun—and much easier to catch something—if you stand in the water.

"Yeah, I'll catch something," he grumbled as he rolled up the cuffs of his jeans. "I'll catch pneumonia!"

Stanley let out a loud laugh. It sounded like, "Har! Har! Har!"

He set the big picnic basket down carefully on the dry grass. Then he rolled up the legs of his denim overalls. Carrying a rod high in one hand, he stepped into the water.

"Ooooh! It's cold!" he cried, waving his arms above his head, nearly losing his balance on the slippery rocks.

"Stanley—didn't you forget something?" I called to him.

He turned, confused. His big ears became bright red. "What did I forget, Jodie?"

I pointed to his fishing rod. "How about some bait?" I called.

He glanced at the empty hook on the end of his line. Then he made his way back to shore to get a worm to bait his hook.

A few minutes later, all three of us were in the water. Mark complained at first about how cold it was and about how the rocks on the bottom hurt his delicate little feet.

But after a while, he got into it, too.

The creek at this point was only about two feet deep. The water was very clear and trickled rapidly, making little swirls and dips over the rocky bottom.

I lowered my line into the water and watched the red plastic float bob on the surface. If it started to sink, I'd know I had a bite.

The sun felt warm on my face. The cool water flowed past pleasantly.

I wish it were deep enough to swim here, I thought.

"Hey—I've got something!" Mark cried excitedly.

Stanley and I turned and watched him tug up his line.

Mark pulled with all his might. "It—it's a big one, I think," he said.

Finally, he gave one last really hard tug—and pulled up a thick clump of green weeds.

"Good one, Mark," I said, rolling my eyes. "It's a big one, all right."

"*You're* a big one," Mark shot back. "A big jerk."

"Don't be such a baby," I muttered.

I brushed away a buzzing horsefly and tried to concentrate on my line. But my mind started to wander. It always does when I'm fishing.

162

I found myself thinking about the tall scarecrows in the field. They stood so darkly, so menacingly, so alert. Their painted faces all had the same hard stare.

I was still picturing them when I felt the hand slip around my ankle.

The straw scarecrow hand.

It reached up from the water, circled my ankle, and started to tighten its cold, wet grip around my leg.

I screamed and tried to kick the hand away.

But my feet slipped on the smooth rocks. My hands shot up as I toppled backwards.

"Ohh!" I cried out again as I hit the water.

The scarecrow hung on.

On my back, the water rushing over me, I kicked and thrashed my arms.

And then I saw it. The clump of green weeds that had wrapped itself around my ankle.

"Oh, no," I moaned out loud.

No scarecrow. Only weeds.

I lowered my foot to the water. I didn't move. I just lay there on my back, waiting for my heart to stop pounding, feeling once again like a total jerk.

I glanced up at Mark and Stanley. They were staring down at me, too startled to laugh.

"Don't say a word," I warned them, struggling to my feet. "I'm warning you—don't say a word."

Mark sniggered, but he obediently didn't say anything.

"I didn't bring a towel," Stanley said with concern. "I'm sorry, Jodie, I didn't know you wanted to swim."

That made Mark burst out in loud guffaws.

I shot Mark a warning stare. My T-shirt and shorts were soaked. I started to shore, carrying the rod awkwardly in front of me.

"I don't need a towel," I told Stanley. "It feels good. Very refreshing."

"You scared away all the fish, Jodie," Mark complained.

"No. *You* scared them away. They saw your *face!*" I replied. I knew I was acting like a baby now. But I didn't care. I was cold and wet and angry.

I stomped on to the shore, shaking water from my hair.

"I think they're biting better down here," I heard Stanley call to Mark. I turned to see him disappear around a curve of the creek.

Stepping carefully over the rocks, Mark followed after him. They were both hidden from view behind the thick trees.

I squeezed my hair, trying to get the creek water out. Finally, I gave up and tossed my hair behind my shoulder.

I was debating what to do next when I heard a crackling sound in the woods.

A footstep?

I turned and stared into the trees. I couldn't see anyone.

Another chipmunk scurried away over the blanket of dead, brown leaves. Had someone—or some*thing*—frightened the chipmunk?

I listened hard. Another crackling footstep. Rustling sounds.

"Who—who's there?" I called.

The low bushes rustled in reply.

"Sticks—is that you? Sticks?" My voice trembled.

No reply.

It *has* to be Sticks, I told myself. This is Grandpa Kurt's property. No one else would be back here.

"Sticks—stop trying to scare me!" I shouted angrily.

No reply.

Another footstep. The crack of a twig.

More rustling sounds. Closer now.

"Sticks—I know it's you!" I called uncertainly. "I'm really tired of your stupid tricks. Sticks?"

My eyes stared straight ahead into the trees.

I listened. Silence now.

Heavy silence.

And then I raised my hand to my mouth as I saw the dark figure poke out from the shade of two tall pines.

"Sticks—?"

166

I squinted into the deep blue shadows.

I saw the bulging, dark coat. The faded sack head. The dark fedora hat tilted over the black, painted eyes.

I saw the straw poking out under the jacket. The straw sticking out from the long jacket sleeves.

A scarecrow.

A scarecrow that had followed us? Followed us to the creek?

Squinting hard into the shadows, staring at its evil, frozen grin, I opened my mouth to scream—but no sound came out.

And then a hand grabbed my shoulder.

"Ohh!" I let out a cry and spun around.

Stanley stared at me with concern. He and Mark had come up behind me.

"Jodie, what's the matter?" Stanley asked. "Mark and I—we thought we heard you calling."

"What's up?" Mark asked casually. The line on his fishing rod had become tangled, and he was working to untangle it. "Did you see a squirrel or something?"

"No—I—I—" My heart was pounding so hard, I could barely speak.

"Chill out, Jodie," Mark said, imitating me.

"I saw a scarecrow!" I finally managed to scream.

Stanley's mouth dropped open.

Mark narrowed his eyes suspiciously at me. "A scarecrow? Here in the woods?"

"It—it was walking," I stammered. "I heard it. I heard it walking."

A choking sound escaped Stanley's open mouth.

Mark continued to stare at me, his features tight with fear.

"It's over there!" I cried. "Right there! Look!" I pointed.

But it was gone.

Stanley stared hard at me, his big brown eyes filled with confusion.

"I saw it," I insisted. "Between those two trees." I pointed again.

"You did? A scarecrow? Really?" Stanley asked. I could see he was really starting to get scared.

"Well . . . maybe it was just the shadows," I said. I didn't want to frighten Stanley.

I shivered. "I'm soaked. I've got to get back in the sunlight," I told them.

"But did you see it?" Stanley asked, his big eyes locked on mine. "Did you see a scarecrow here, Jodie?"

"I—I don't think so, Stanley," I replied, trying to calm down. "I'm sorry."

"This is very bad," he murmured, talking to himself. "This is very bad. I have to read the book. This is very bad." Then, muttering to himself, he turned and ran.

170

"Stanley—stop!" I called. "Stanley—come back! Don't leave us down here!"

But he was gone. Vanished into the woods.

"I'm going after him," I told Mark. "And then I'm going to tell Grandpa Kurt about this. Can you carry back the fishing rods by yourself?"

"Do I have to?" Mark whined. My brother is so lazy!

I told him he had to. Then I went running along the path through the woods towards the farmhouse.

My heart pounded as I reached the cornfields. The dark-coated scarecrows appeared to stare at me. As my sneakers thudded on the narrow dirt path, I imagined the straw arms reaching for me, reaching to grab me and pull me into the corn.

But the scarecrows kept their silent, still watch over the cornstalks. They didn't move or twitch as I hurtled past.

Up ahead I saw Stanley running to his little house. I cupped my hands over my mouth and called to him, but he disappeared inside.

I decided to find Grandpa Kurt and tell him about the scarecrow I'd seen moving through the woods.

The barn door was open, and I thought I saw someone moving around inside. "Grandpa Kurt?" I called breathlessly. "Are you in there?"

My wet hair bounced on my shoulders as I ran

171

into the barn. I stood in the rectangle of light that stretched from the doorway and stared into the darkness. "Grandpa Kurt?" I called, struggling to catch my breath.

My eyes slowly adjusted to the dim light. I stepped deeper into the barn. "Grandpa Kurt? Are you here?"

Hearing a soft scraping sound against the far wall, I made my way towards it. "Grandpa Kurt—can I talk to you? I really need to talk to you!" My voice sounded tiny and frightened in the big, dark barn. My trainers scraped over the dry straw floor as I walked towards the back.

I spun around as I heard a rumbling sound.

The light grew dimmer.

"Hey—" I shouted. Too late.

The barn door was sliding shut.

"Hey! Who's there?" I cried out in stunned anger. "Hey—stop!"

I slipped over the straw as I started to lurch towards the sliding door. I fell down hard, but quickly scrambled to my feet.

I darted towards the door. But I wasn't fast enough.

As the heavy door rumbled shut, the rectangle of light grew narrower, narrower.

The door slammed with a deafening *bang*.

The darkness slid around me, circled me, covered me.

"Hey—let me out!" I screamed. "Let me out of here!"

My scream ended in a choked sob. My breath escaped in noisy gasps.

I pounded on the wooden barn door with both fists. Then I frantically swept my hands over the door, searching blindly for a latch, for something to pull—some way to open the door.

When I couldn't find anything, I pounded on the door until my fists hurt.

Then I stopped and took a step back.

Calm down, Jodie, I told myself. Calm down. You'll get out of the barn. You'll find a way out. It's not like you're trapped in here for ever.

I tried to force away my panic. I held my breath, waiting for my heart to stop racing. Then I let my breath out slowly. Slooooowly.

I was just starting to feel a little better when I heard the scraping sound.

A dry scraping. The sound of a shoe crunching over straw.

"Oh." I let out a sharp cry, then raised both hands to my face and listened.

Scrape. Scrape. Scrape.

The sound of footsteps. Slow, steady footsteps, so light on the barn floor.

Footsteps coming towards me in the darkness.

173

11

"Who—who's there?" I choked out, my voice a hushed whisper.

No reply.

Scrape. Scrape. Scrape.

The soft, scratchy footsteps came closer.

"Who *is* it?" I cried shrilly.

No reply.

I stared into the darkness. I couldn't see a thing.

Scrape. Scrape.

Whoever—or whatever—was moving steadily towards me.

I took a step back. Then another.

I tried to cry out, but my throat was choked with fear.

I let out a terrified gasp as I backed into something. In my panic, it took me a few seconds to realize that it was only a wooden ladder. The ladder that led up to the hayloft.

The footsteps crunched closer. Closer.

"Please—" I uttered in a tiny, choked voice. "Please—don't—"

Closer. Closer. Scraping towards me through the heavy darkness.

I gripped the sides of the ladder. "Please—leave me alone!"

Before I realized what I was doing, I was pulling myself up the ladder. My arms trembled, and my legs felt as if they each weighed a thousand kilos.

But I scrambled rung by rung towards the hayloft, away from the frightening, scraping footsteps down below.

When I reached the top, I lay flat on the hayloft floor. I struggled to listen, to hear the footsteps over the loud pounding of my heart.

Was I being followed? Was the thing chasing me up the ladder?

I held my breath. I listened.

Scrabbling sounds. Scraping footsteps.

"Go away!" I screamed frantically. "Whoever you are—go away!"

But the sounds continued, dry and scratchy. Like straw brushing against straw.

Scrambling to my knees, I turned to the small, square hayloft window. Sunlight filtered in through the window. The light made the hay strewn over the floor gleam like slender strands of gold.

My heart still pounding, I crawled to the window.

Yes! The heavy rope was still tied to the side. The rope that Mark and I always used to swing down to the ground.

I can get out of here! I told myself happily.

I can grab the rope and swing out of the hayloft. I can escape!

Eagerly, I grabbed the rope with both hands.

Then I poked my head out of the window and gazed down to the ground.

And let out a scream of surprise and horror.

Gazing down, I saw a black hat. Beneath it, a black coat.

A scarecrow. Perched outside the barn door. As if standing guard.

It jerked its arms and legs at the sound of my scream.

And as I stared in disbelief, it hurried around the side of the barn, hobbling on its straw legs, its arms flapping at its sides.

I blinked several times.

Was I *seeing* things?

My hands were cold and wet. I gripped the rope more tightly. Taking a deep breath, I plunged out of the small square window.

The heavy rope swung out over the front of the barn.

Down, down. I hit the ground hard, landing on my feet.

"Ow!" I cried out as the rope cut my hands.

I let go and ran around to the side of the barn. I

wanted to catch up with that scarecrow. I wanted to see if it really was a scarecrow, a scarecrow that could run.

Ignoring my fear, I ran as fast as I could.

No sign of him on this side of the barn.

My chest began to ache. My temples throbbed.

I turned the corner and headed around the back of the barn, searching for the fleeing scarecrow.

And ran right into Sticks!

"Hey—" We both shouted in surprise as we collided.

I frantically untangled myself from him. Staring past him, I saw that the scarecrow had vanished.

"What's the hurry?" Sticks demanded. "You practically ran me over!"

He was wearing faded denim jeans, slashed at both knees, and a faded purple muscle shirt that only showed off how skinny he was. His black hair was tied back in a short ponytail.

"A—a scarecrow!" I stammered.

And, then—that instant—I knew.

In that instant, I solved the whole mystery of the scarecrows.

It hadn't been a scarecrow.

It was Sticks.

In the woods down by the creek. And, now, outside the barn.

Sticks. Playing another one of his mean tricks.

And I was suddenly certain that Sticks had somehow made the scarecrows twitch and pull on their stakes last night.

Sticks just loved fooling the "city kids". Ever since Mark and I had been little, he'd played the scariest, meanest practical jokes on us.

Sometimes Sticks could be a nice guy. But he had a really cruel streak.

"I thought you were fishing," he said casually.

"Well, I'm not," I snapped. "Sticks, why do you keep trying to scare us?"

"Huh?" He pretended he didn't know what I was talking about.

"Sticks, give me a break," I muttered. "I know you were the scarecrow just now. I'm not stupid!"

"Scarecrow? What scarecrow?" he asked, giving me a wide-eyed, innocent expression.

"You were dressed as a scarecrow," I accused him. "Or else you carried one here, and pulled it on a string or something."

"You're totally crazy," Sticks replied angrily. "Have you been out in the sun too long or something?"

"Sticks—give up," I said. "Why are you doing this? Why do you keep trying to scare Mark and me? You scared your dad, too."

"Jodie, you're nuts!" he exclaimed. "I really don't have time to be dressing up in costumes just to amuse you and your brother."

"Sticks—you're not fooling me," I insisted. "You—"

I stopped short when I saw Sticks's expression change. "Dad!" he cried, suddenly frightened. "Dad! You say he was scared?"

I nodded.

"I've got to find him!" Sticks exclaimed frantically. "He—he could do something *terrible*!"

"Sticks, your joke has gone far enough!" I cried. "Just *stop* it!"

But he was already running towards the front of the barn, calling for his father, his voice shrill and frantic.

Sticks didn't find his dad until dinnertime. That's the next time I saw him, too—just before dinner. He was carrying his big superstition book, holding it tightly under his arm.

"Jodie," he whispered, motioning for me to come close. His face was red. His dark eyes revealed his excitement.

"Hi, Stanley," I whispered back uncertainly.

"Don't tell Grandpa Kurt about the scarecrow," Stanley whispered.

"Huh?" Stanley's request caught me off guard.

"Don't tell your grandpa," Stanley repeated. "It will only upset him. We don't want to frighten him, do we?"

"But, Stanley—" I started to protest.

Stanley raised a finger to his lips. "Don't tell, Jodie. Your grandpa doesn't like to be upset. I'll take care of the scarecrow. I have the book." He tapped the big book with his finger.

I started to tell Stanley that the scarecrow was only Sticks, playing a mean joke. But Grandma Miriam called us to the table before I could get the words out.

Stanley carried his superstition book to the table. Every few bites, he would pick up the big, black book and read a few paragraphs.

He moved his lips as he read. But I was sitting down at the other end of the table and couldn't make out any of the words.

Sticks kept his eyes down on his plate and hardly said a word. I think he was really embarrassed that his father was reading the superstition book at the dinner table.

But Grandpa Kurt and Grandma Miriam didn't seem the least bit surprised. They talked cheerfully to Mark and me and kept passing us more food—as if they hadn't even noticed Stanley's behaviour.

I really wanted to tell Grandpa Kurt about how Sticks was trying to scare Mark and me. But I decided to listen to Stanley and not upset my grandfather.

Besides, I could deal with Sticks if I had to. He thought he was so tough. But I wasn't the least bit afraid of him.

Stanley was still reading, jabbering away as he read, as Grandma Miriam cleared the dinner dishes. Mark and I helped. Then we took our seats as Grandma Miriam carried a big cherry pie to the table.

"Weird," Mark whispered to me, staring at the pie.

He was right. "Doesn't Grandpa Kurt like *apple* pie?" I blurted out.

Grandma Miriam gave me a tense smile. "Too early in the year for apples," she murmured.

"But isn't Grandpa Kurt allergic to cherries?" Mark asked.

Grandma Miriam started cutting the pie with a silver pie cutter. "Everyone loves cherry pie," she replied, concentrating on her work. Then she raised her eyes to Stanley. "Isn't that right, Stanley?"

Stanley grinned over his book. "It's my favourite," he said. "Grandma Miriam always serves my favourite."

After dinner, Grandpa Kurt once again refused to tell Mark and me a scary story.

We were sitting around the fireplace, staring at the crackling yellow flames. Even though it had been so hot, the air had grown cool this evening, cool enough to build a nice, toasty fire.

Grandpa Kurt was in his rocking chair at the side of the hearth. The old wooden chair creaked as he rocked slowly back and forth.

He had always loved to gaze at the fire and tell us one of his frightening stories. You could see the leaping flames reflected in his blue eyes. And his voice would go lower and lower as the story got scarier.

But tonight he shrugged when I asked him for a story. He stared dully at the huge stuffed bear on its pedestal against the wall. Then he glanced across the room at Stanley.

"Wish I knew some good stories," Grandpa Kurt replied with a sigh. "But I've clean run out."

A short while later, Mark and I trudged upstairs to our bedrooms. "What is his problem?" Mark whispered as we climbed.

I shook my head. "Beats me."

"He seems so . . . different," Mark said.

"Everyone here does," I agreed. "Except for Sticks. He's still trying to scare us city kids."

"Let's just ignore him," Mark suggested. "Let's just pretend we don't see him running around in his stupid scarecrow costume."

I agreed. Then I said good night and headed into my room.

Ignore the scarecrows, I thought as I arranged the blankets on the bed.

Just ignore them.

I'm not going to think about scarecrows again, I told myself.

Sticks can go jump in the creek.

Climbing into bed, I pulled the quilt up to my chin. I lay on my back, staring up at the cracks in the ceiling, trying to figure out what kind of picture they formed. There were three jagged cracks. I decided they looked like bolts of lightning.

If I squinted, I could make them look like an old man with a beard.

I yawned. I felt really sleepy, but I couldn't get to sleep.

It was only my second night here at the farm. It always takes me a while to adjust to being in a new place and sleeping in a different bed.

I closed my eyes. Through the open window, I could hear the soft mooing of cows from the

184

barn. And I could hear the whisper of the wind as it brushed through the tall cornstalks.

My nose was totally stuffed up. Bet I snore tonight, I thought.

That is, if I ever get to sleep!

I tried counting sheep. It didn't seem to be working, so I tried counting cows. Big, bulky, bouncing, slooooooow-mooooooving cows.

I counted to a hundred and twelve before I decided that wasn't working, either.

I turned on to my side. Then, after a few minutes, I tried my other side.

I found myself thinking about my best friend, Shawna. I wondered if Shawna was having a good time at camp.

I thought about some of my other friends. Most of them were just hanging around this summer, not doing much of anything.

When I glanced at the clock, I was surprised to see it was nearly twelve. I've *got* to get to sleep, I told myself. I'll be *wrecked* tomorrow if I don't get some sleep.

I settled on to my back, pulling the soft quilt up to my chin again. I closed my eyes and tried to picture nothing. Just empty, black space. Endless, empty space.

The next thing I knew, I was hearing scratching sounds.

I ignored them at first. I thought the curtains were flapping against the open window.

Got to get to sleep, I urged myself. *Got to get to sleep*.

The scratching grew louder. Closer.

I heard a scraping sound.

From outside the window?

I opened my eyes. Shadows danced on the ceiling. I realized I was holding my breath.

Listening hard.

Another scrape. More scratching. Dry scratching.

I heard a low groan.

"Huh?" A startled gasp escaped my lips.

I pulled myself up against the headboard. I tugged the quilt up to my chin, gripping it tightly with both hands.

I heard more dry scraping. Like sandpaper, I thought.

Suddenly the room grew darker.

I saw something pull itself up to the window. A dark figure. Blocking the moonlight.

"Who—who's there?" I tried to call. But my voice came out a choked whisper.

I could see a shadowy head, black against the purple sky.

It rose up in the window. Dark shoulders. Followed by a darker chest. Black against black.

A silent shadow, slipping into my room.

"H-help!" Another stammered whisper.

My heart had stopped beating. I couldn't breathe. Couldn't breathe.

It slid over the window-sill. Brushed away the curtains as it lowered itself into my room.

Its feet scraped over the bare floorboards.

Scratch scratch scratch.

It moved slowly, steadily towards my bed.

I struggled to get up.

Too late.

My feet tangled in the quilt.

I fell to the floor, landing hard on my elbows.

I raised my eyes to see it move closer.

I opened my mouth to scream as it emerged from the shadows.

And then I recognized him. Recognized his face.

"Grandpa Kurt!" I cried. "Grandpa Kurt—what are you doing here? Why did you climb in the window?"

He didn't reply. His cold blue eyes glared down at me. His whole face twisted into an ugly frown.

And then he raised both arms above me.

And I saw that he had no hands.

Clumps of straw poked out from his jacket sleeves.

Only straw.

"Grandpa—*no!*" I shrieked.

"Grandpa—*please*—*no*!" I shrieked as he lowered his straw arms towards me.

He bared his teeth like an angry dog and let out a sharp, frightening growl.

The straw hands reached down for me.

Grandpa Kurt's face was the same. The face I had always known. Except that his eyes were so cold, so cold and dead.

The straw hands brushed over my face as I climbed to my feet. I took a step back, raising my hands like a shield.

"Grandpa—what's wrong? What's happening?" I whispered.

My temples were pounding. My entire body shook.

His cold eyes narrowed in fury as he reached for me again.

"Noooo!" I let out a long wail of terror. Then I turned and stumbled to the door.

His feet scraped over the bare floor as he

lurched towards me. Glancing down, I saw the straw poking out from the cuffs of his trousers.

His feet—they were straw, too.

"Grandpa Kurt! Grandpa Kurt! What is *happening*?" Was that really my voice, so shrill and frightened?

He swung an arm. The straw scratched my back as it swept over me.

I grabbed for the doorknob. Twisted it. Pulled open the door.

And cried out again as I collided with Grandma Miriam.

"Oh, help! Please help! Grandma Miriam—he's *chasing* me!" I cried.

Her expression didn't change. She stared back at me.

In the dim light of the hallway, her face came into focus.

And I saw that her glasses were *painted* on.

And her eyes. And mouth. And big round nose.

Her entire face was painted on.

"You're not real!" I cried.

And then darkness swept over me as Grandpa Kurt's straw hands wrapped around my face.

I woke up coughing and choking.

Surrounded by darkness. Heavy darkness.

It took me a few seconds to realize that I'd been sleeping with the pillow over my face.

Tossing it to the foot of the bed, I pulled myself up, breathing hard. My face was hot. My night-shirt stuck wetly to my back.

I glanced at the window, suddenly afraid that I'd see a dark figure climbing in.

The curtains fluttered gently. The early morning sky was still grey. I heard the shrill cry of a rooster.

A dream. It had all been a frightening nightmare.

Taking a deep breath and letting it out slowly, I lowered my feet to the floor.

I stared at the grey morning light through the window. Just a dream, I assured myself. Calm down, Jodie. It was just a dream.

I could hear someone moving around

downstairs. Staggering over to the dresser, I pulled out some fresh clothes—a pair of faded denim cut-offs, a sleeveless blue T-shirt.

My eyes were watery. Everything was a blur. My allergies were really bad this morning.

Rubbing my eyes, I made my way to the window and peered out. A red ball of a sun was just peeking over the broad apple tree. A heavy morning dew made the grass of the back yard sparkle like emeralds.

The sea of cornstalks rose darkly behind the grass. The scarecrows stood stiffly over them, arms outstretched as if welcoming the morning.

The rooster crowed again.

What a stupid nightmare, I thought. I shook myself as if trying to shake it from my memory. Then I ran a brush through my hair and hurried down to breakfast.

Mark was just entering the kitchen as I came in. We found Grandma Miriam by herself at the table. A mug of tea steamed in front of her as she gazed out of the window at the morning sunlight.

She turned and smiled at us as we entered. "Good morning. Sleep well?"

I was tempted to tell her about my scary nightmare. But, instead, I asked, "Where's Grandpa Kurt?" I stared at his empty chair. The newspaper lay unopened on the table.

191

"They all went off early," Grandma Miriam replied.

She stood up, walked to the cabinets, and brought a big box of cornflakes to the table. She motioned for us to take our places. "Pretty day," she said cheerfully.

"No pancakes?" Mark blurted out.

Grandma Miriam stopped half-way across the room. "I've completely forgotten how to make them," she said without turning around.

She put two bowls down and made her way to the refrigerator to get the milk. "You kids want orange juice this morning? It's freshly squeezed."

Grandma Miriam put the milk carton down beside my bowl. She smiled at me. Her eyes remained dull behind her square-rimmed glasses. "I hope you two are enjoying your visit," she said quietly.

"We would be if it weren't for Sticks," I blurted out.

Her expression turned to surprise. "Sticks?"

"He's trying to scare us again," I said.

Grandma Miriam tsk-tsked. "You know Sticks," she replied softly.

She pushed at her red hair with both hands. "What are you two planning for today?" she asked brightly. "It's a beautiful morning to go riding. Before they left this morning, Grandpa Kurt got Stanley to saddle up Betsy and Maggie, in case you wanted to ride."

"Sounds like fun," I told her. "What do you say, Mark? Before it gets really hot out?"

"All right," Mark replied.

"You two always enjoyed riding along the creek," Grandma Miriam said, putting the cornflakes box away.

I stared across the room at her, stared at her red, curly hair, her pudgy arms, her flowered dress.

"Are you okay, Grandma Miriam?" I asked. The words just tumbled out of my mouth. "Is everything okay here?"

She didn't reply. Instead, she lowered her eyes, avoiding my gaze. "Go and have your ride," she said quietly. "Don't worry about me."

Grandpa Kurt always called Betsy and Maggie the "old grey mares". I guess because they were both old and they were both grey. And they were as grumpy as can be when Mark and I climbed on to their saddles and started to urge them from the barn.

They were the perfect horses for us "city kids". The only time we ever got to ride horses was during our summers at the farm. So we were not exactly the most skilful riders in the world.

Bumping along on these two old nags was just our speed. And even as slow as we were moving, I dug my knees into Betsy's sides and held on to the saddle horn for dear life.

We followed the dirt track past the cornfields towards the woods. The sun was still climbing in the hazy, yellow sky. But the air was already hot and sticky.

Flies buzzed around me as I bounced on top of Betsy. I removed one hand from the saddle horn to brush a big one off Betsy's back.

Several scarecrows stared back at us as Mark and I rode past. Their black eyes glared at us from under their floppy hats.

Mark and I didn't say a word. We were keeping to our promise of not talking about scarecrows.

I turned my eyes to the woods and tossed the reins, urging Betsy to move a little faster. She ignored me, of course, and kept clopping along the path at her slow, steady pace.

"I wonder if these horses can still get up to a trot," Mark called. He was a few paces behind me on the narrow dirt track.

"Let's give it a try!" I called back, grabbing the reins tighter.

I dug the heels of my trainers into Betsy's side. "Go, girl—go!" I cried, slapping her gently with the reins.

"Whoooa!" I let out a startled cry as the old horse obediently began to trot. I really didn't think she would cooperate!

"All *right*! Cool!" I heard Mark shout behind me.

Their hooves clopped loudly on the path as the two horses began to pick up speed. I was bouncing hard over the saddle, holding on tightly, off-balance, beginning to wonder if this was such a hot idea.

I didn't have a chance to try to cry out when the dark figure hurtled across the path.

It all happened so fast.

Betsy was trotting rapidly. I was bouncing on the saddle, bouncing so hard, my feet slipped out of the stirrups.

The dark figure leaped out right in front of us.

Betsy let out a shrill, startled whinny—and reared back.

As I started to fall, I saw immediately what had jumped on to the path.

It was a grinning scarecrow.

Betsy rose up with a high whinny.

My hand grabbed for the reins, but they slipped from my grasp.

The sky appeared to roll over me, then tilt away.

I slid backwards, out of the saddle, off the horse, my feet thrashing wildly for the flapping stirrups.

The sky tilted even more.

I hit the ground hard on my back.

I remember only the shock of stopping so abruptly, the surprise at how hard the ground felt, how so much pain shot through my body so quickly.

The sky turned bright red. A glowing scarlet. Like an explosion.

And then the scarlet faded to deep, deep, endlessly deep black.

I heard low moans before I opened my eyes.

I recognized the voice. Mark's voice.

My eyes still shut, I opened my mouth to call to him. My lips moved, but no sound came out.

"Ohhhh." Another low groan from him, not far from me.

"Mark—?" I managed to choke out. My back ached. My shoulders hurt. My head throbbed. Everything hurt.

"My wrist—I think I've broken it," Mark said, his voice shrill and frightened.

"You fell, too?" I asked.

"Yeah. I fell, too," he groaned.

I opened my eyes. Finally. I opened my eyes. And saw the hazy sky.

All a blur. Everything was a watery blur.

I stared at the sky, trying to get it in focus.

And then saw a hand in front of the sky. A hand lowering itself towards me.

A bony hand stretching out from a heavy black coat.

The hand of the scarecrow, I realized, staring up helplessly at it.

The hand of the scarecrow, coming down to grab me.

The hand grabbed my shoulder.

Too terrified to cry out, too dazed to think clearly, my eyes followed the dark coat sleeve—up to the shoulder—up to the face.

A blur. All a frightening blur.

And then the face became clear.

"Stanley!" I cried.

He leaned over me, his red ears glowing, his face tight with worry. He gently grabbed my shoulder. "Jodie—are you all right?"

"Stanley—it's you!" I exclaimed happily. I sat up. "I think I'm okay. I don't know. Everything hurts."

"What a bad fall," Stanley said softly. "I was in the field. And I saw it. I saw the scarecrow . . ."

His voice trailed off. I followed his frightened gaze up ahead of me on the path.

The scarecrow lay face down across the path.

"I saw it jump out," Stanley uttered with

a shudder that shook his whole body.

"My wrist . . ." Mark moaned from nearby.

I turned as Stanley hurried over to him. Mark was sitting up in the grass at the side of the path, holding his wrist. "Look—it's starting to swell up," he groaned.

"Oooh, that's bad. That's bad," Stanley said, shaking his head.

"Maybe it's just a sprain," I suggested.

"Yeah," Stanley quickly agreed. "We'd better get you to the house and put ice on it. Can you get back up on Maggie? I'll ride behind you."

"Where's *my* horse?" I asked, searching both ways along the path. I climbed unsteadily to my feet.

"She galloped back to the barn," Stanley replied, pointing. "Fastest I've ever seen her go in years!"

He glanced down at the scarecrow and shuddered again.

I took a few steps, stretching my arms and my back. "I'm okay," I told him. "Take Mark on the horse. I'll walk back."

Stanley eagerly started to help Mark to his feet. I could see that Stanley wanted to get away from here—away from the scarecrow—as fast as possible.

I watched as they rode off down the path towards the house. Stanley sat behind Mark in the saddle, holding the reins, keeping Maggie at a slow, gentle pace. Mark held his wrist against his chest and leaned back against Stanley.

I stretched my arms over my head again, trying to stretch the soreness from my back. My head ached. But other than that, I didn't feel bad.

"Guess I'm lucky," I murmured out loud.

I took a long glance at the scarecrow, sprawled face down across the path. Cautiously, I walked over to it.

I poked its side with the toe of my trainer.

The straw beneath the coat crinkled.

I poked it harder, pushing my trainer hard into the scarecrow's middle.

I don't know what I expected to happen. Did I think the scarecrow would cry out? Try to squirm away?

With an angry cry, I kicked the scarecrow. Hard.

I kicked it again.

The sack head bounced on the path. The scarecrow's ghastly painted grin didn't move.

It's just a scarecrow, I told myself, giving it one last kick that sent straw falling out from the jacket front.

Just a scarecrow that Sticks tossed on to the path.

Mark and I could have been killed, I told myself.

We're lucky we weren't.

Sticks. It had to be Sticks.

But why?

This wasn't a joke.

Why was Sticks trying to *hurt* us?

18

Stanley and Sticks weren't at lunch. Grandpa Kurt said they had to go into town for supplies.

Mark's wrist was only sprained. Grandma Miriam put an ice bag on it, and the swelling went right down. But Mark was groaning and complaining. He was really making the most of it.

"Guess I'll have to lie on the couch and watch TV for a week or so," he moaned.

Grandma Miriam served ham sandwiches and home-made coleslaw. Mark and I gobbled down our lunches. All that excitement had made us really hungry.

As we ate, I decided to tell Grandpa Kurt everything that had been happening. I couldn't hold it in any longer.

I told him about how Sticks was making the scarecrows move at night. And how he was trying to frighten us, trying to make us think the scarecrows were alive.

I caught a glimpse of fear in Grandpa Kurt's blue eyes. But then he rubbed his white-stubbled cheeks, and he got a faraway look on his face.

"Sticks and his little jokes," he said finally, a smile spreading across his face. "That boy sure likes his jokes."

"He's not joking," I insisted. "He's really trying to frighten us, Grandpa."

"We could have been killed this morning!" Mark joined in. He had mayonnaise smeared on his cheek.

"Sticks is a good boy," Grandma Miriam murmured. She was smiling, too. She and Grandpa Kurt exchanged glances.

"Sticks wouldn't really hurt you," Grandpa Kurt said softly. "He just likes to have his fun."

"Great fun!" I muttered sarcastically, rolling my eyes.

"Yeah. Great fun," Mark groaned. "I almost broke my wrist!"

Grandpa Kurt and Grandma Miriam just smiled back at us, their faces frozen like the painted scarecrow faces.

After lunch, Mark slumped on the couch, where he planned to spend the rest of the afternoon staring at the TV. He *loved* having an excuse not to go outdoors.

I heard Stanley's truck pull up the drive. I decided to go and find Sticks and tell him how fed up we were with his stupid scarecrow tricks.

I didn't think his jokes were all in fun. I really believed he was trying to frighten us or hurt us—and I wanted to find out why.

I didn't see Sticks or Stanley out in the yard. So I made my way across the grass to the guest house where they lived.

It was a warm, beautiful day. The sky was clear and bright. The air smelled fresh and sweet.

But I couldn't enjoy the sunshine. All I could think about was letting Sticks know how angry I was.

I knocked on the guest house door. I took a deep breath and tossed my hair behind my shoulders, listening for signs of life inside.

I tried to think of what I was going to say to Sticks. But I was too angry to plan it. My heart started to pound. I realized I was breathing hard.

I knocked on the door again, harder this time. There was no one inside.

I turned my gaze into the cornfields. The stalks stood stiffly, watched over by the motionless scarecrows. No sign of Sticks.

I turned to the barn, across the wide grass from the guest house. Maybe Sticks is in there, I thought.

I jogged to the barn. Two enormous crows hopped along the ground in front of the open barn doors. They flapped their wings hard and scrambled out of my way.

"Hey—Sticks?" I shouted breathlessly as I stepped inside.

No reply.

The barn was dark. I waited for my eyes to adjust.

Remembering my last creepy visit to the barn, I stepped reluctantly, my trainers scraping over the straw on the floor. "Sticks? Are you in here?" I called, staring hard into the deep shadows.

A rusted baling machine stood to one side of the straw bales. A wheelbarrow tilted against the wall. I hadn't noticed them before.

"Guess he isn't here," I said to myself out loud.

I walked past the wheelbarrow. I saw something else I hadn't noticed before—a pile of old coats on the barn floor. Empty sacks were stacked beside them.

I picked one up. It had a frowning face painted on it in black paint. I dropped the bag back on to the pile.

These must be Stanley's scarecrow supplies, I realized.

How many more scarecrows did he plan to build?

Then something in the corner caught my eye. I walked quickly over the straw. Then I bent down to examine what I saw.

Torches. At least a dozen torches, stacked in

the corner, hidden by the darkness. Next to them I spotted a large bottle of kerosene.

What on earth are *these* doing here? I asked myself.

Suddenly, I heard a scraping sound. I saw shadows slide against shadows.

And I realized that once again I was no longer alone.

I jumped to my feet. "Sticks!" I cried. "You scared me."

His face was half hidden in darkness. His black hair fell over his forehead. He didn't smile. "I warned you," he said menacingly.

Feeling the fear rise to my throat, I stepped out of the corner and moved past him, into the light from the doorway. "I—I was looking for you," I stammered. "Sticks, why are you trying to scare Mark and me?"

"I warned you," he said, lowering his voice to a whisper. "I warned you to get away from here, to go back home."

"But why?" I demanded. "What's your problem, Sticks? What did we do to you? Why are you trying to scare us?"

"I'm not," Sticks replied. He glanced back nervously to the barn doors.

"Huh?" I gaped at him.

"I'm not trying to scare you. Really," he insisted.

"Liar," I muttered angrily. "You must really think I'm a moron. I *know* you threw that scarecrow on to our path this morning. It had to be you, Sticks."

"I really don't know what you're talking about," he insisted coldly. "But I'm warning you—"

A sound at the doorway made him stop.

We both saw Stanley step into the barn. He shielded his eyes with one hand as his eyes adjusted to the darkness. "Sticks—are you in here?" he called.

Sticks's features tightened in sudden fear. He let out a low gasp.

"I—I've got to go," Sticks whispered tensely to me. He turned and started jogging towards Stanley. "Here I am, Dad," he called. "Is the tractor ready?"

I watched the two of them hurry from the barn. Sticks didn't look back.

I stood in the darkness, my eyes on the empty doorway, thinking hard.

I *know* Sticks was lying to me, I thought.

I *know* he made the scarecrows move at night. I know he dressed as a scarecrow to scare me in the woods and at the barn. And I know he tossed that scarecrow in front of the horses this morning.

I know he's trying to frighten Mark and me.

But enough is enough, I decided.

Now it's payback time.

Now it's time for *Sticks* to be frightened. Really frightened.

"I can't do this!" Mark protested.

"Of course you can," I assured him. "This is going to be really cool."

"But my wrist hurts again," my brother whined. "It's just started hurting. I can't use it."

"No problem," I told him. "You won't have to use it."

He started to protest some more. But then a smile spread across his face, and his eyes lit up gleefully. "It's kind of a cool idea," he said, laughing.

"Of *course* it's an awesome idea," I agreed. "*I* thought of it!"

We were standing in the doorway to the barn. The white light from a full moon shone down on us. Owls hooted somewhere nearby.

It was a cool, clear night. The grass shimmered from a heavy dew. A soft wind made the trees whisper. The moonlight was so bright, I could see every blade of grass.

After Grandpa Kurt and Grandma Miriam had gone to bed, I dragged Mark from the house. I pulled him across the yard to the barn.

"Wait right here," I said. Then I hurried into the barn to get what we needed.

It was a little creepy in the dark barn at night. I heard a soft fluttering sound high in the rafters.

Probably a bat.

My trainers were wet from the grass. I slid over the straw on the barn floor.

The bat swooped low over my head. I heard a high-pitched chittering up in the rafters. More bats.

I grabbed one of the big, old coats from the pile. Then I pulled up one of the sack faces and slung it on top of the coat.

Ignoring the fluttering wings swooping back and forth, back and forth, across the barn, I hurried outside to Mark.

And explained my plan, my plan to get our revenge on Sticks.

It was actually a very simple plan. We'd dress Mark up as a scarecrow. He'd stand with the other scarecrows in the cornfields.

I'd go to the guest house and get Sticks. I'd tell Sticks I'd seen something weird in the field. I'd pull Sticks out to the field. Mark would start to stagger towards him—and Sticks would be so freaked, he'd have a cow!

A simple plan. And a good one.

Sticks deserved it, too.

I pulled the sack over Mark's head. The black, painted eyes stared back at me. I reached down, picked up a handful of straw, and began stuffing it under the bag.

"Stop squirming!" I told Mark.

"But the straw itches!" he cried.

"You'll get used to it," I told him. I grabbed his shoulders. "Stand still. Don't move."

"Why do I need straw?" he whined.

"Mark, you have to look like all the other scarecrows," I told him. "Otherwise, Sticks won't be fooled."

I stuffed the sack face with straw. Then I held up the old overcoat for Mark to put on.

"I can't do this!" he wailed. "I'm going to itch to death! I can't breathe!"

"You can breathe perfectly fine," I told him. I stuffed straw into the sleeves. I was careful to let clumps of straw hang from the cuffs, covering Mark's hands. Then I stuffed more straw into the jacket.

"Will you stand still?" I whispered angrily. "This is a lot of hard work—you know?"

He grumbled in a low voice to himself as I continued to work.

"Just keep thinking how great it'll be when Sticks sees you and thinks you're a scarecrow that's really coming to life," I said.

211

I had straw stuck to my hands, straw all down the front of my sweatshirt and jeans. I sneezed. Once. Twice. I'm definitely allergic to the stuff.

But I didn't care. I was so excited. I couldn't *wait* to see Sticks's terrified face. I couldn't *wait* to pay him back for trying to frighten us all week.

"I need a hat," Mark said. He was standing stiffly, afraid to move under all the straw.

"Hmmmm." I thought hard. There weren't any hats in the barn with the other scarecrow supplies. "We'll just take one off a real scarecrow," I told Mark.

I stepped back to see my handiwork. Mark looked pretty good. But he still needed more straw. I set to work, stuffing him, making the old coat bulge.

"Now don't forget to stand straight and stiff, with your arms straight out," I instructed.

"Do I have a choice?" Mark complained. "I—I can't move at all!"

"Good," I said. I arranged the straw that stuck out of his sleeves, then stepped back. "Okay. You're ready," I told him.

"How do I look?" he asked.

"Like a short scarecrow," I told him.

"I'm too short?" he replied.

"Don't worry, Mark," I said, grabbing his arm. "I'm going to stick you up on a pole!"

"Huh?"

I laughed. "Gotcha," I muttered. "I'm kidding." I started to lead him to the cornfields.

"Think this is going to work?" Mark asked, walking stiffly. "Think we're really going to scare Sticks?"

I nodded. An evil grin spread over my face. "I think so," I told my brother. "I think Sticks is in for a terrifying surprise."

Little did I know that we *all* were!

I gripped Mark's arm with both hands and led him to the cornfields. The bright moon bathed us in white light. The tall cornstalks shivered in a light breeze.

Mark looked so much like a scarecrow, it was scary. Tufts of straw stuck out at his neck and the cuffs of his coat. The enormous old coat hung loosely over his shoulders and came down nearly to his knees.

We stepped into the field. Our trainers crunched over the dry ground as we edged through a narrow row.

The cornstalks rose above our heads. The breeze made them lean over us, as if trying to close us in.

I let out a gasp as I heard a rustling sound along the ground.

Footsteps?

Mark and I both froze. And listened.

The tall stalks bent low as the wind picked

up. They made an eerie creaking sound as they moved. The ripe corn sheaths bobbed heavily.

Creeeeak. Creeeeak.

The stalks shifted back and forth.

Then we heard the rustling again. A soft brushing sound.

Very nearby.

"Ow. Let go!" Mark whispered.

I suddenly realized I was still gripping his arm, squeezing it tightly.

I let go. And listened. "Can you hear it?" I whispered to Mark. "That brushing sound?"

Creeeeak. Creeeeak.

The cornstalks leaned over us, shifting in the wind.

A twig cracked. So close to me, I nearly jumped out of my skin.

I held my breath. My heart was racing.

Another soft rustling sound. I stared down at the ground, trying to follow the sound.

"Oh."

A large grey squirrel scampered across the row and disappeared between the stalks.

I burst out laughing, mostly from relief. "Just a squirrel," I said. "Do you believe it? Just a squirrel!"

Mark let out a long, relieved sigh from under the sack. "Jodie, can we get going?" he demanded impatiently. "This thing itches like crazy!"

He raised both hands and tried to scratch his face through the sack. But I quickly tugged his arms down. "Mark—stop. You'll mess up the straw!"

"But my face feels like a hundred bugs are crawling all over it!" he wailed. "And I can't see. You didn't cut the eyeholes big enough."

"Just follow me," I muttered. "And stop complaining. You want to scare Sticks, don't you?"

Mark didn't reply. But he let me lead him deeper into the cornfield.

Suddenly, a black shadow fell over our path.

I let out a sharp gasp before I realized it was the long shadow of a scarecrow.

"How do you do," I said, reaching out and shaking its straw hand. "May I borrow your hat?"

I reached up and pulled the brown, floppy hat off the sack head. Then I lowered it over Mark's sack head and pulled it down tight.

"Hey—!" Mark protested.

"I don't want it to fall off," I told him.

"I'm never going to stop itching!" Mark whined. "Can you scratch my back? *Please?* My whole back is itching!"

I gave the back of the old coat a few hard rubs. "Turn around," I instructed him. I gave him a final inspection.

216

Excellent. He looked more like a scarecrow than the scarecrows did.

"Stand right here," I told him, moving him into a small clearing between two rows of cornstalks. "Good. Now when you hear me bringing Sticks over, put your arms straight out. And don't move a muscle."

"I know, I know," Mark grumbled. "Think I don't know how to be a scarecrow? Just hurry—okay?"

"Okay," I told him. I turned and made my way quickly along the shifting rows of cornstalks. Dry straw and leaves crackled beneath my trainers.

I was breathing hard by the time I reached the guest house. The doorway was dark. But an orange light glowed dimly behind the pulled shade in the window.

I hesitated at the doorway and listened. Silence inside.

How was I going to get Sticks to come out alone—without his father?

I didn't want to frighten Stanley. He was a really nice man, who would never think of playing mean jokes on Mark and me. And I knew how scared and upset he could get.

I only wanted to frighten Sticks. To teach him a lesson. To teach him he had no business getting on our case just because Mark and I are "city kids".

217

The wind fluttered through my hair. I could hear the cornstalks creaking behind me in the fields.

I shivered.

Taking a deep breath, I raised my fist to knock on the door.

But a sound behind me made me spin around.

"Hey—!" I choked out.

Someone was moving across the grass, half running, half stumbling. My eyes were all watery. It was hard to see.

Was it Mark?

Yes. I recognized the floppy hat, the bulky, dark overcoat falling down past his knees.

What is he doing? I asked myself, watching him approach.

Why is he following me?

He's going to ruin the whole joke!

As he came closer, he raised a straw hand as if pointing at me.

"Mark—what's wrong?" I called in a loud whisper.

He continued to gesture with his straw hands as he ran.

"Mark—get back in the field!" I whispered. "You're not supposed to follow me. You're going to ruin everything! Mark—what are you *doing* here?"

I motioned with both hands for him to go back to the cornfield.

But he ignored me and kept coming, trailing straw as he ran.

"Mark, please—go back! Go back!" I pleaded.

But he stepped up in front of me and grabbed my shoulders.

And as I stared into the cold, painted black eyes—I realized to my horror that *it wasn't Mark!*

I cried out and tried to pull away.

But the scarecrow held on to me tightly.

"Sticks—is that you?" I cried in a trembling voice.

No reply.

I stared into the blank, painted eyes.

And realized there were no human eyes behind them.

The straw hands scratched against my throat.

I opened my mouth to scream.

And the door to the guest house swung open. "Sticks—" I managed to choke out.

Sticks stepped out on to the small step. "What on earth—!" he cried.

He leaped off the step, grabbed the scarecrow by the coat shoulders—and heaved it to the ground.

The scarecrow hit the ground without making a sound. It lay sprawled on its back, staring up at us blankly.

"Who—who is it?" I cried, rubbing my neck where the straw hands had scratched it.

Sticks bent down and jerked away the sack scarecrow head.

Nothing underneath. Nothing but straw.

"It—it really is a scarecrow!" I cried in horror. "But it—*walked*!"

"I warned you," Sticks said solemnly, staring down at the headless dark figure. "I warned you, Jodie."

"You mean it wasn't you?" I demanded. "It wasn't you trying to scare Mark and me?"

Sticks shook his head. He raised his dark eyes to mine. "Dad brought the scarecrows to life," he said softly. "Last week. Before you came. He used his book. He chanted some words—and they all came to life."

"Oh, no," I murmured, raising my hands to my face.

"We were all so frightened," Sticks continued. "Especially your grandparents. They begged Dad to recite the words and put the scarecrows back to sleep."

"Did he?" I asked.

"Yes," Sticks replied. "He put them back to sleep. But first he insisted your grandparents make some promises. They had to promise not to laugh at him any more. And they had to promise to do everything he wanted from now on."

Sticks took a deep breath. He stared towards

the guest house window. "Haven't you noticed how different things are at the farm? Haven't you noticed how frightened your grandparents are?"

I nodded solemnly. "Of course I have."

"They've been trying to keep Dad happy," Sticks continued. "They've been doing everything they can to keep him from getting upset or angry. Your grandmother only makes his favourite food. Your grandfather has stopped telling scary stories because Dad doesn't like them."

I shook my head. "They're *that* afraid of Stanley?"

"They're afraid he'll read the chant in the book again and bring the scarecrows back to life," Sticks said. He swallowed hard. "There's only one problem," he murmured.

"What's that?" I asked.

"Well, I haven't told Dad yet. But . . ." His voice trailed off.

"But what?" I demanded eagerly.

"Some of the scarecrows are still alive," Sticks replied. "Some of them never went back to sleep."

We both let out short cries as the front door to the house swung open.

Startled, I leaped away from the doorway.

As the door pulled open, it revealed a rectangle of orange light. Stanley stepped into the light.

He held on to the door and peered out. His eyes showed surprise as they landed on Sticks and me. But then he goggled and uttered a choking sound as he spotted the headless scarecrow on the ground.

"N-no!" Stanley sputtered. He pointed a trembling finger at the scarecrow. "It—it walks! The scarecrow walks!"

"No, Dad—!" Sticks cried.

But Stanley didn't hear him. Stanley had already dived back into the house.

Sticks started after him. But Stanley reappeared in the doorway. As he stepped outside, I saw that he was carrying the big superstition book.

"The scarecrows walk!" Stanley screamed. "I must take charge! I must take charge of them all now!"

His eyes were wild. His entire skinny body was trembling. He started towards the cornfields, totally crazy. Sticks tried to calm him down.

"No, Dad!" Sticks cried desperately, hurrying after him. "The scarecrow was dropped here! I dropped it here, Dad! It didn't walk! It didn't walk!"

Stanley kept walking, taking long, rapid strides. He didn't seem to hear Sticks. "I must take charge now!" Stanley declared. "I must be the leader. I will bring the others back to life and take control."

He turned and glanced at Sticks, who was hurrying to catch up to him. "Stay back!" Stanley shouted. "Stay back—until I read the chant! Then you can follow!"

"Dad—please listen to me!" Sticks cried. "The scarecrows are all asleep! Don't wake them!"

Stanley finally stopped a few yards from the edge of the cornfields. He turned to Sticks and studied his face. "You're sure? You're sure they're not out of my control? You're sure they're not walking?"

Sticks nodded. "Yes. I'm sure, Dad. I'm really sure."

Stanley's face filled with confusion. He kept staring hard at Sticks, as if not believing him. "I don't have to read the chant?" Stanley asked, confused, his eyes on the swaying cornstalks. "I don't have to take charge?"

"No, Dad," Sticks replied softly. "The scarecrows are all still. You can put the book away. The scarecrows are not moving."

Stanley sighed with relief. He lowered the book to his side. "None of them?" he asked warily.

"None of them," Sticks replied soothingly.

And that's when Mark—in full scarecrow costume—decided to come staggering out of the cornfield.

"Where've you been?" Mark called.

Stanley's eyes went wide, and he opened his mouth in a high shriek of terror.

"Dad, please—!" Sticks pleaded.

Too late.

Stanley took off, heading into the corn-fields, the big book raised high in front of him. "The scarecrows walk! They walk!" he cried.

Mark tugged at the sack face. "Did we blow it?" he called. "Is the joke over? What's happening?"

There was no time to answer him.

Sticks turned to me, his features tight with fear. "We've got to stop Dad!" he cried. He started running to the swaying cornstalks.

Stanley had already disappeared between the tall rows of corn.

My allergies were really bad. I kept rubbing my eyes, trying to clear them. But as I followed

Sticks, everything was a shimmering blur of greys and blacks.

"Ow!" I cried out as I stumbled in a soft hole and fell.

Mark, right behind me, nearly toppled over me.

He reached down and helped pull me up. I had landed hard on both knees, and they were throbbing with pain.

"Which way did they go?" I asked breathlessly, searching the dark, swaying rows of creaking cornstalks.

"I—I'm not sure!" Mark stammered. "What's going on, Jodie? Tell me!"

"Not now!" I told him. "We have to stop Stanley. We have to—"

Stanley's voice, high and excited, rose up from somewhere nearby. Mark and I both froze as we listened to the strange words he was chanting.

"Is he reading something from that weird book?" Mark demanded.

Without answering, I headed in the direction of Stanley's voice. It was easy to follow him. He was chanting the strange words at the top of his lungs.

Where was Sticks? I wondered.

Why hadn't Sticks been able to stop his father?

I pushed frantically through the tall stalks. I was moving blindly, my eyes watered over, brushing the stalks out of the way with both hands.

In a small clearing, I found Stanley and Sticks. They were standing in front of two scarecrows on poles.

Stanley held the book up close to his face as he chanted, moving his finger over the words.

Sticks stood frozen, a blank expression on his face, a face of cold terror.

Had the words of the chant somehow frozen him there like that?

The scarecrows stood stiffly on their poles, their painted eyes staring lifelessly out from under their floppy black hats.

Mark and I stepped into the clearing just as Stanley finished his chant. He slammed the big book shut and tucked it under one arm.

"They're going to walk now!" Stanley cried excitedly. "They're going to come alive again!"

Sticks suddenly seemed to come back to life. He blinked several times and shook his head hard, as if trying to clear it.

We all stared at the two scarecrows.

They stared back at us, lifeless, unmoving.

The clouds floated away from the moon. The shadow over the cornfields rolled away.

I stared into the eerie, pale light.

A heavy silence descended over us. The only sounds I could hear were Stanley's shallow breathing, tense gasps as he waited for his chant to work, for his scarecrows to come to life.

I don't know how long we stood there, none of us moving a muscle, watching the scarecrows. Watching. Watching.

"It didn't work," Stanley moaned finally. His voice came out sad and low. "I did something wrong. The chant—it didn't work."

A smile grew on Sticks's face. He gazed at me. "It didn't work!" Sticks exclaimed happily.

And then I heard the *scratch scratch scratch* of dry straw.

I saw the scarecrows' shoulders start to twitch. I saw their eyes light up and their heads lean forward.

Scratch scratch scratch.

The dry straw crinkled loudly as they both squirmed off their poles and lowered themselves silently to the ground.

"Go and warn your grandparents!" Sticks cried. "Hurry! Go and tell them what my dad has done!"

Mark and I hesitated. We stared at the scarecrows as they stretched their arms and rolled their sack heads, as if waking up after a long sleep.

"Jodie—look!" Mark choked out in a hushed whisper. He pointed out to the fields.

I gasped in horror as I saw what Mark was staring at.

All over the field, dark-coated scarecrows were stretching, squirming, lowering themselves from their poles.

More than a dozen of them, silently coming to life.

"Run!" Sticks was screaming. "Go! Tell your grandparents!"

Stanley stood frozen in place, gripping the book in both hands. He stared in amazement, shaking his head, enjoying his triumph.

Sticks's face was knotted with fear. He gave my shoulders a hard shove. "Run!"

The scarecrows were rolling their heads back and forth, stretching out their straw arms. The dry scratch of straw filled the night air.

I forced myself to take my eyes off them. Mark and I turned and started running through the cornfield. We pushed the tall stalks away with both hands as we ran. We ducked our heads low, running in terrified silence.

We ran across the grass, past the guest house. Past the dark, silent barn.

The farmhouse loomed darkly ahead of us. The windows were dark. A dim porch light sent a circle of yellow light over the back porch.

"Hey—!" Mark shouted, pointing.

Grandpa Kurt and Grandma Miriam must have heard our shouts back in the cornfields. They were waiting for us in the back yard.

They looked frail and frightened. Grandma Miriam had pulled a flannel bathrobe over her nightdress. She had a scarf tied over her short red hair.

Grandpa Kurt had pulled his overalls on over his pyjamas. He leaned heavily on his stick, shaking his head as Mark and I came running up.

"The scarecrows—!" I exclaimed breathlessly.

"They're walking!" Mark cried. "Stanley— he—"

"Did you get Stanley upset?" Grandpa Kurt asked, his eyes wide with fear. "Who got Stanley upset? He promised us he wouldn't do it again! He promised—if we didn't upset him."

"It was an accident!" I told him. "We didn't mean to. Really!"

"We've worked so hard to keep Stanley happy," Grandma Miriam said sadly. She chewed her lower lip. "So hard . . ."

"I didn't think he'd do it," Grandpa Kurt said, his eyes on the cornfields. "I thought we convinced him it was too dangerous."

"Why are you dressed like that?" Grandma Miriam asked Mark.

I was so frightened and upset, I had completely forgotten that Mark was still dressed as a scarecrow.

"Mark, did you dress like that to scare Stanley?" Grandma Miriam demanded.

"No!" Mark cried. "It was supposed to be a joke! Just a joke!"

"We were trying to scare Sticks," I told them. "But when Stanley saw Mark, he . . ."

My voice trailed off as I saw the dark figures step out of the cornfields.

In the silvery moonlight, I saw Stanley and Sticks. They were running hard, leaning forwards as they ran. Stanley held the book in front of him. His shoes slipped and slid over the wet grass.

Behind them came the scarecrows. They were moving awkwardly, staggering, lurching silently forward.

Their straw arms stretched straight forward, as if reaching to grab Stanley and Sticks. Their round, black eyes glowed blankly in the moonlight.

Staggering, tumbling, falling, they came after Stanley and Sticks. A dozen twisted figures in black coats and hats. Leaving clumps of straw as they pulled themselves forward.

Grandma Miriam grabbed my arm and squeezed it in terror. Her hand was as cold as ice.

We watched Stanley fall, then scramble to his feet. Sticks helped pull him up, and the two of them continued to run towards us in terror.

The silent scarecrows lurched and staggered closer. Closer.

"Help us—*please!*" Stanley called to us.

"What can we do?" I heard Grandpa Kurt mutter sadly.

The four of us huddled close together, staring in helpless horror as the scarecrows made their way, chasing Stanley and Sticks across the moonlit lawn.

Grandma Miriam held on to my arm. Grandpa Kurt leaned heavily, squeezing the handle of his stick.

"They won't obey me!" Stanley screamed breathlessly. He stopped in front of us, holding the book in one hand.

His chest was heaving up and down as he struggled to catch his breath. Despite the coolness of the night, sweat poured down his forehead.

"They won't obey me! They *must* obey me! The book says so!" Stanley cried, frantically waving the book in the air.

Sticks stopped beside his father. He turned to watch the scarecrows approach. "What are you going to do?" he asked his father. "You *have* to do something!"

"They're alive!" Stanley shrieked. "Alive!"

"What does the book say?" Grandpa Kurt demanded.

"They're alive! They're all alive!" Stanley repeated, his eyes wild with fright.

"Stanley—listen to me!" Grandpa Kurt yelled. He grabbed Stanley by the shoulders and spun him around to face him. "Stanley—what does the book say to do? How do you get them in control?"

"Alive," Stanley murmured, his eyes rolling in his head. "They're all alive."

"Stanley—what does the book say to do?" Grandpa Kurt demanded once again.

"I—I don't know," Stanley replied.

We turned back to the scarecrows. They were moving closer. Spreading out. Forming a line as they staggered towards us. Their arms reached forward menacingly, as if preparing to grab us.

Clumps of straw fell from their sleeves. Straw spilled from their coats.

But they continued to lurch towards us. Closer. Closer.

The black, painted eyes stared straight ahead. They leered at us with their ugly, painted mouths.

"Stop!" Stanley screamed, raising the book high over his head. "I command you to stop!"

The scarecrows lurched slowly, steadily forward.

"Stop!" Stanley shrieked in a high, frightened voice. "I brought you to life! You are mine! Mine! I command you! I command you to stop!"

The blank eyes stared straight at us. The arms reached stiffly forward. The scarecrows pulled themselves closer. Closer.

"Stop! I said *stop!*" Stanley screeched.

Mark edged closer to me. Behind his sack mask I could see his eyes. Terrified eyes.

Ignoring Stanley's frightened pleas, the scarecrows dragged themselves closer. Closer.

And then I did something that changed the whole night.

I sneezed.

27

Mark was so startled by my sudden, loud sneeze that he let out a short cry and jumped away from me.

To my amazement, the scarecrows all stopped moving forward—and jumped back, too.

"Whoa!" I cried. "What's going on here?"

The scarecrows all seemed to have trained their painted eyes on Mark.

"Mark—quick—raise your right hand!" I cried.

Mark gazed at me through the sack. I could see confusion in his eyes.

But he obediently raised his right hand high over his head.

And the scarecrows all raised *their* right hands!

"Mark—they're imitating you!" Grandma Miriam cried.

Mark raised *both* hands in the air.

The scarecrows copied him again. I heard the

scratch of straw as they lifted both arms.

Mark tilted his head to the left. The scarecrows tilted their heads to the left.

Mark dropped to his knees. The scarecrows sank in their straw, slaves to my brother's every move.

"They—they think you're one of them," Grandpa Kurt whispered.

"They think you're their *leader*!" Stanley cried, staring wide-eyed at the scarecrows slumped on the ground.

"But how do I make them go back to their poles?" Mark demanded excitedly. "How do I make them go back to being scarecrows?"

"Dad—find the right chant!" Sticks yelled. "Find the right words! Make them sleep again!"

Stanley scratched his short, dark hair. "I— I'm too scared!" he confessed sadly.

And then I had an idea.

"Mark—" I whispered, leaning close to him. "Pull off your head."

"Huh?" He gazed at me through the sack mask.

"Pull off your scarecrow head," I urged him, still whispering.

"But why?" Mark demanded. He waved his hands in the air. The scarecrows obediently waved their straw hands in the air.

Everyone was staring at me, eager to hear my explanation.

"If you pull off your scarecrow head," I told Mark, "then they will pull off *their* heads. And they'll die."

Mark hesitated. "Huh? You think so?"

"It's worth a try," Grandpa Kurt urged.

"Go ahead, Mark. Hurry!" Sticks cried.

Mark hesitated for a second. Then he stepped forward, just inches from the dark-coated scarecrows.

"Hurry!" Sticks urged him.

Mark gripped the top of the sack with both hands. "I sure hope this works," he murmured. Then he gave the sack a hard tug and pulled it off.

The scarecrows stopped moving. They stood still as statues as they watched Mark pull off his scarecrow head.

Mark stared back at them, holding the sack between his hands. His hair was matted wetly to his forehead. He was dripping with sweat.

The scarecrows hesitated for a moment more.

A long, silent moment.

I held my breath. My heart was pounding.

Then I let out a happy cry as the scarecrows all reached up with their straw hands—and pulled off their heads!

The dark hats and sack heads fell silently to the grass.

None of us moved. We were waiting for the scarecrows to fall.

Waiting for the headless scarecrows to collapse and fall.

But they didn't go down.

Instead, they reached out their arms and moved stiffly, menacingly forward.

"They—they're coming to get us!" Stanley cried in a high, trembling voice.

"Mark—*do* something!" I shouted, shoving him forward. "Make them stand on one foot or hop up and down. Stop them!"

The headless figures dragged themselves towards us, arms outstretched.

Mark stepped forward. He raised both hands over his head.

The scarecrows didn't stop, didn't copy him.

"Hey—hands up!" Mark shouted desperately. He waved his hands above his head.

The scarecrows edged forward, silently, steadily.

"Th-they're not doing it!" Mark wailed. "They're not *following* me!"

"You don't look like a scarecrow any more," Grandma Miriam added. "They don't think you're their leader."

Closer they came, staggering blindly. Closer.

They formed a tight circle around us.

A scarecrow brushed its straw hand against my cheek.

I uttered a terrified cry. "Noooooo!"

It reached for my throat, the dry straw scratching me, scratching my face, scratching, scratching.

The headless scarecrows swarmed over Mark.

He thrashed and kicked. But they were smothering him, forcing him to the ground.

My grandparents cried out helplessly as the dark-coated figures surrounded them. Stanley let out a silent gasp.

"Sticks—help me!" I shrieked as the straw hands wrapped around my neck. "Sticks? Sticks?"

I glanced frantically around.

"Sticks? Help me! Please! Where are you?"

Then I realized to my horror that Sticks was gone.

"Sticks?" I let out a final muffled cry.

The straw hands wrapped around my throat. The scarecrow rolled over me. My face was pressed into the dry straw of its chest.

I tried to squirm free. But it held on, surrounded me, choked me.

The straw smelled sour. Decayed. I felt sick. A wave of nausea swept over me.

"Let go! Let go!" I heard Stanley pleading.

The scarecrow was surprisingly strong. It wrapped its arms around me tightly, smothering me in the disgusting straw.

I made one last attempt to pull free. Struggling with all my might, I raised my head.

And saw two balls of fire. Orange streaks of light.

Floating closer.

And in the orange light, I saw Sticks's face, hard and determined.

I gave another hard tug. And tumbled backwards.

"Sticks!" I cried.

He was carrying two blazing torches. The torches from the barn, I realized.

"I was saving these just in case!" Sticks called.

The scarecrows seemed to sense danger.

They let go of us, tried to scramble away.

But Sticks moved quickly.

He swept the two torches, swinging them like baseball bats.

A scarecrow caught fire. Then another.

Sticks made another wide swing.

The fire crackled, a streak of orange against the darkness.

The dry straw burst into flame. The old coats burned quickly.

The scarecrows twisted and writhed as the bright flames danced over them. They sank to their backs on the ground. Burning. Burning so brightly, so silently, so fast.

I took a step back, staring in horror and fascination.

Grandpa Kurt had his arm around Grandma Miriam. They leaned close together, their faces reflecting the flickering flames.

Stanley stood tensely, his eyes wide. He hugged the book tightly to his chest. He was murmuring to himself, but I couldn't make out the words.

Mark and I stood beside Sticks, who held a torch in each hand, watching with narrowed eyes as the scarecrows burned.

In seconds, there was nothing left but clumps of dark ashes on the ground.

"It's over," Grandma Miriam murmured softly, gratefully.

"Never again," I heard Stanley mutter.

The house was quiet the next afternoon.

Mark was out on the screen porch, lying in the hammock, reading a stack of comic books. Grandpa Kurt and Grandma Miriam had gone in for their afternoon nap.

Sticks had driven into town to pick up the mail.

Stanley sat at the kitchen table, reading his superstition book. His finger moved over the page as he muttered the words aloud in a low voice.

"Never again," he had repeated at lunch. "I've learned my lesson about this book. I'll never try to bring any scarecrows to life again. I won't even *read* the part about scarecrows!"

We were all glad to hear that.

So now, on this lazy, peaceful afternoon, Stanley sat at the table, quietly reading some chapter of the big book.

And I sat alone on the couch in the living room, hearing Stanley's gentle murmurings from the kitchen, thinking about the night before.

It felt good to have a quiet afternoon, to be all alone to think about what had happened.

All alone . . .

The only one in the room . . .

The only one to hear Stanley's low mumbling as he read the book.

The only one to see the gigantic stuffed brown bear blink its eyes.

The only one to see the bear lick its lips, step off its platform, snarl and paw the air with its enormous claws.

The only one to hear its stomach growl as it stared down at me.

The only one to see the hungry look on its face as it magically came out of its long hibernation.

"Stanley?" I called in a tiny, high voice. "Stanley? What chapter have you been reading?"

Attack of the Mutant

"Hey—put that down!"

I grabbed the comic book from Wilson Clark's hand and smoothed out the plastic cover.

"I was only looking at it," he grumbled.

"If you get a fingerprint on it, it will lose half its value," I told him. I examined the cover through the clear wrapper. "This is a *Silver Swan* Number Zero," I said. "And it's in mint condition."

Wilson shook his head. He has curly, white-blond hair and round, blue eyes. He always looks confused.

"How can it be Number Zero?" he asked. "That doesn't make any sense, Skipper."

Wilson is a really good friend of mine. But sometimes I think he dropped down from the planet Mars. He just doesn't know *anything*.

I held up the *Silver Swan* cover so he could see the big zero in the corner. "That makes it a collector's item," I explained. "Number Zero

comes before Number One. This comic is worth
ten times as much as *Silver Swan* Number One."

"Huh? It is?" Wilson scratched his curly hair.
He squatted down on the floor and started
pawing through my box of comic books. "How
come all your comics are in these plastic bags,
Skipper? How can you read them?"

See? I told you. Wilson doesn't know anything.

"Read them? I don't read them," I replied. "If
you read them, they lose their value."

He stared up at me. "You don't read them?"

"I can't take them out of the bag," I explained.
"If I open the bag, they won't be in mint
condition any more."

"Ooh. This one is cool!" he exclaimed. He
pulled up a copy of *Star Wolf*. "The cover is
metal!"

"It's worthless," I mumbled. "It's a second
printing."

He stared at the silvery cover, turning it in his
hands, making it shine in the light. "Cool," he
muttered. His favourite word.

We were up in my room, about an hour after
dinner. The sky was black outside my double
windows. It gets dark so early in winter. Not like
on the Silver Swan's planet, Orcos III, where the
sun never sets and all the superheroes have to
wear air-conditioned costumes.

Wilson had come over to get the maths homework. He lives next door, and he always leaves

his maths book at school—so he always comes over to get the homework from me.

"You should collect comic books," I told him. "In about twenty years, these will be worth millions."

"I collect rubber stamps," he said, picking up a *Z-Squad* annual. He studied the trainer ad on the back cover.

"Rubber stamps?"

"Yeah. I have about a hundred of them," he said.

"What can you do with rubber stamps?" I asked.

He dropped the comic back into the box and stood up. "Well, you can stamp things with them," he said, brushing off the knees of his jeans. "I have different-coloured ink pads. Or you can just look at them."

He is definitely weird.

"Are they valuable?" I asked.

He shook his head. "I don't think so." He picked up the maths sheet from the foot of my bed. "I'd better get home, Skipper. See you tomorrow."

He started for the door and I followed him. Our reflections stared out at us from my big dressing-table mirror. Wilson is so tall and skinny and blond and blue-eyed. I always feel like a dark, chubby mole next to him.

If we were in a comic book, Wilson would be

the superhero, and I would be his sidekick. I'd be the pudgy, funny one who was always messing up.

It's a good thing life isn't a comic book—right?

As soon as Wilson left, I turned back to my dressing-table. My eye caught the big computer banner above the mirror: SKIPPER MATTHEWS, ALIEN AVENGER.

My dad had got someone at his office to print out the banner for me for my twelfth birthday a few weeks ago.

Beneath the banner, I have two great posters tacked on the wall on both sides of the dressing-table. One is a Jack Kirby *Captain America*. It's really old and probably worth about a thousand dollars.

The other one is newer—a *Spawn* poster by Todd McFarlane. It's really awesome.

In the mirror, I could see the excited look on my own face as I hurried to the dressing-table.

The flat brown envelope waited for me on the dressing-table.

Mum and Dad said I couldn't open it until after dinner, after I finished my homework. But I couldn't wait.

I could feel my heart start to pound as I stared down at the envelope.

I knew what waited inside it. Just thinking about it made my heart pound even harder.

I carefully picked up the envelope. I had to open it now. I *had* to.

Carefully, carefully, I tore the flap on the envelope. Then I reached inside and pulled out the treasure.

This month's issue of *The Masked Mutant*.

Holding the comic book in both hands, I studied the cover. *The Masked Mutant 24*. In jagged red letters across the bottom, I read:

"A TIGHT SQUEEZE
FOR THE SENSATIONAL SPONGE!"

The cover art was awesome. It showed SpongeLife—known across the universe as The Sponge of Steel—in terrible trouble. He was caught in the tentacles of a gigantic octopus. The octopus was squeezing him dry!

Awesome. Totally awesome.

I keep all of my comic books in mint condition, wrapped in collector's bags. But there is one comic that I have to read every month. And that's *The Masked Mutant*.

I have to read it as soon as it comes out. And I

read it cover to cover, every word in every panel. I even read the Letters page.

That's because *The Masked Mutant* is the best-drawn, best-written comic in the world. And The Masked Mutant *has* to be the most powerful, most evil villain ever created!

What makes him so terrifying is that he can move his molecules around.

That means he can change himself into anything that's solid. *Anything!*

On this cover, the giant octopus is actually The Masked Mutant. You can tell because the octopus is wearing the mask that The Masked Mutant always wears.

But he can change himself into *any* animal. Or any object.

That's how he always escapes from The League of Good Guys. There are six different superheroes in The League of Good Guys. They are all mutants, too, with amazing powers. And they are the world's best law enforcers. But they can't catch The Masked Mutant.

Even the League's leader—The Galloping Gazelle—the fastest man in the solar system, isn't fast enough to keep up with The Masked Mutant.

I studied the cover for a few minutes. I liked the way the octopus tentacles squeezed Sponge-Life into a limp rag. You could see by his expression that The Sponge of Steel was in mortal pain.

Awesome.

I carried the comic over to the bed and sprawled on to my stomach to read it. The story began where *The Masked Mutant 23* left off.

SpongeLife, the world's best underwater swimmer, was deep in the ocean. He was desperately trying to escape from The Masked Mutant. But The Sponge of Steel had caught his cape on the edge of a coral reef.

I turned the page. As The Masked Mutant drew nearer, he began to move his molecules around. And he changed himself into a huge, really gross octopus.

There were eight drawings showing The Masked Mutant transform himself. And then came a big, full-page drawing showing the enormous octopus reaching out its slimy, fat tentacles to grab the helpless SpongeLife.

SpongeLife struggled to pull away.

But the octopus tentacles slid closer. Closer.

I started to turn the page. But before I could move, I felt something cold and slimy wrap itself around *my* neck.

I let out a gasp and tried to struggle free.

But the cold tentacles wrapped themselves tighter around my throat.

I couldn't move. I couldn't scream.

I heard laughter.

With a great effort, I turned around. And saw Mitzi, my nine-year-old sister. She pulled her hands away from my neck and jumped back as I glared at her.

"Why are your hands so cold?" I demanded.

She smiled at me with her innocent, two-dimpled smile. "I put them in the refrigerator."

"You *what*?" I cried. "You put them in the refrigerator? Why?"

"So they'd be cold," she replied, still grinning.

My sister has a really stupid sense of humour. She has straight, dark brown hair like me. And she's short and a little chubby like me.

"You scared me to death," I told her, sitting up on the bed.

"I know," she replied. She rubbed her hands on my cheeks. They were still cold.

"Yuck. Get away, Mitzi." I shoved her back. "Why did you come up here? Just to scare me?"

She shook her head. "Dad told me to come up. He said to tell you if you're reading comic books instead of doing your homework, you're in big trouble."

She lowered her brown eyes to the comic book, open on the bed. "Guess you're in big trouble, Skipper."

"No. Wait." I grabbed her arm. "This is the new *Masked Mutant*. I *have* to read it! Tell Dad I'm doing my maths, and—"

I didn't finish what I was saying because my dad stepped into the room. The ceiling light reflected in his glasses. But I could still see that he had his eyes on the open comic book on my bed.

"Skipper—" he said angrily in his booming, deep voice.

Mitzi pushed past him and ran out of the room. She liked to cause trouble. But she never wanted to stay around once things got *really* ugly.

And I knew things were about to get ugly— because I had already been warned three times that week about spending too much time with my comic book collection.

"Skipper, do you know why your grades are so bad?" my dad bellowed.

257

"Because I'm not a very good student?" I replied.

A mistake. Dad hates it when I answer back.

Dad reminds me of a big bear. Not only because he growls a lot. But because he is big and broad. He has short, black hair and almost no forehead. Really. His hair starts almost right above his glasses. And he has a big, booming roar of a voice, like a bear's roar.

Well, after I answered him back, he let out an angry roar. Then he lumbered across the room and picked up my box of comic books—my entire collection.

"Sorry, Skipper, I'm throwing all these out!" he cried, and headed for the door.

You probably expected me to panic. To start begging and pleading for him not to throw away my valuable collection.

But I didn't say anything. I just stood beside the bed with my hands lowered at my sides, and waited.

You see, Dad has done this before. Lots of times. But he doesn't really mean it.

He has a bad temper, but he's no supervillain. Actually, I'd put him in The League of Good Guys most of the time.

His main problem is that he doesn't approve of comic books. He thinks they're just trash. Even when I explain that my collection will probably be worth millions by the time I'm his age.

Anyway, I stood there and waited silently.

Dad stopped at the door and turned around. He held the box in both hands. He narrowed his dark eyes at me through his black-framed glasses.

"Are you going to get to your work?" he asked sternly.

I nodded. "Yes, sir," I muttered, staring at my feet.

He lowered the box a little. It's really heavy, even for a big, strong guy like him. "And you won't waste any more time tonight on comic books?" he demanded.

"Couldn't I just finish this new one?" I asked. I pointed to *The Masked Mutant* comic on the bed.

Another mistake.

He growled at me and turned to carry the box away.

"Okay, okay!" I cried. "Sorry. I'll get my homework done, Dad. I promise. I'll start right now."

He grunted and stepped back into the room. Then he dropped the box back against the wall. "That's all you think about night and day, Skipper," he said quietly. "Comics, comics. It isn't healthy. Really. It isn't."

I didn't say anything. I knew he was about to go back downstairs.

"I don't want to hear any more about comics," Dad said gruffly. "Understand?"

"Okay," I murmured. "Sorry, Dad."

I waited to hear his heavy footsteps going down the stairs. Then I turned back to the new issue of *The Masked Mutant*. I was desperate to find out how SpongeLife escaped from the giant octopus.

But I could hear Mitzi nearby. She was still upstairs. If she saw me reading the comic book, she'd run downstairs and tell Dad for sure. Mitzi's hobby is being a snitch.

So I opened my backpack and started pulling out my maths notebook and my science text book and other stuff I needed.

I zipped through the maths questions as fast as I could. I probably got most of the problems wrong. But it doesn't matter. I'm not any good at maths, anyway.

Then I read the chapter on atoms and molecules in my science text book. Reading about molecules made me think about The Masked Mutant.

I couldn't wait to get back to the comic book.

I finally finished my homework a little after nine-thirty. I had to skip a few essay questions on the literature homework. But only the class brains answer *all* of the questions!

I went downstairs and got myself a bowl of Frosted Flakes, my favourite late-night snack. Then I said good night to my parents and hurried back up to my room, closing the door behind me, eager to get back in bed and start reading.

Back under the ocean. SpongeLife escaped by squishing himself so small, he slipped out of the octopus's tentacles. Pretty cool, I thought.

The Masked Mutant waved his tentacles angrily and vowed he'd get SpongeLife another day. Then he changed his molecules back so he looked like himself, and flew back to his headquarters.

His headquarters!

I stared down at the comic book in shock.

The secret headquarters of The Masked Mutant had never been shown before. Oh, sure, we'd been given glimpses of a room or two on the inside.

But this was the first time the building had ever been shown from the outside.

I brought the page up close to my face and examined it carefully. "What a weird place!" I exclaimed out loud.

The headquarters building didn't look like any building I had ever seen before. It certainly didn't look like the secret hideout of the world's worst villain.

It looked a bit like a giant fire hydrant. A very tall fire hydrant that reached up to the sky. All pink stucco with a huge, green-domed roof.

"Weird," I repeated.

But of course it was the perfect hiding place. Who would ever think that the super bad guy of all time stayed in a building that looked like an enormous pink fire hydrant?

I turned the page. The Masked Mutant slipped

262

into the building and disappeared into a lift. He rode all the way to the top and stepped out into his private communications centre.

Waiting for him there was . . . a big surprise. A dark figure. We could see only his black silhouette.

But I could tell instantly who it was. It was The Galloping Gazelle, leader of The League of Good Guys.

How did The Gazelle get in? What was he about to do?

To be continued next month.

Wow. I closed the comic. My eyelids felt heavy. My eyes were too tired to read the tiny type on the Letters page. I decided to save it for tomorrow.

Yawning, I carefully set the comic book down on my bed table. I fell asleep before my head hit the pillow.

Two days later, a very cold, clear day, Wilson came running up to me after school. His blue coat was unzipped. He never zipped his coat. He didn't like the way it looked when it was zipped.

I had on a shirt, a sweater, and a heavy, quilted, down coat, zipped up to my chin—and I was still cold. "What's up, Wilson?" I asked.

His breath steamed up in front of him.

"Want to come over and see my rubber stamp collection?"

Was he *kidding*?!

"I have to go to my orthodontist," I told him. "My brace has got comfortable. He has to tighten it so it'll hurt again."

Wilson nodded. His blue eyes matched his coat. "How are you getting there?"

I pointed to the bus stop. "City bus," I told him.

"I've seen you take that bus a lot," he said.

"There's a comic book shop on Goodale Street," I replied, shifting my backpack on to the other shoulder. "I take the bus there once a week or so to see what new comics have come out. The orthodontist is just a few blocks from it."

"Do they have rubber stamps at the comic book store?" Wilson asked.

"I don't think so," I told him. I saw the blue-and-white city bus turn the corner. "Got to run. See you later!" I called.

I turned and ran full speed to the bus stop.

The driver was a nice guy. He saw me running and waited for me. Breathing hard, I thanked him and climbed on to the bus.

I probably wouldn't have thanked him if I had known where this bus was going to take me. But I didn't know that it was carrying me to the most frightening adventure of my life.

The bus was unusually crowded. I stood for a while. Then two people got off, and I slid into a seat.

As the bus bounced along Main Street, I stared out at the passing houses and front yards. Dark clouds hung low over the roofs. I wondered if we were about to get our first snowfall of the winter.

The comic book shop was a few blocks away. I checked my watch, thinking maybe I had time to stop there before my orthodontist appointment. But no. No time for comics today.

"Hey, do you go to Franklin?" A girl's voice interrupted my thoughts.

I turned to see that a girl had taken the seat beside me. Her carrot-coloured hair was tied back in a single plait. She had green eyes and light freckles on her nose.

She wore a heavy, blue-and-red-plaid ski sweater over faded jeans. She held her red canvas backpack in her lap.

"Yeah. I go there," I replied.

"How is it?" she asked. She narrowed her green eyes at me as if checking me out.

"It's okay," I told her.

"What's your name?" she asked.

"Skipper," I told her.

She sniggered. "That's not a real name, is it?"

"It's what everyone calls me," I said.

"Do you live on a boat or something?" she asked. Her eyes crinkled up. I could see she was laughing at me.

I guess Skipper is a bit of a stupid name. But I've got used to it. I like it a lot better than my real name—Bradley.

"When I was a little kid, I was always in a hurry," I told her. "So I used to skip a lot. That's why they started calling me Skipper."

"Cute," she replied with a smirk.

I don't think I like this girl, I told myself. "What's your name?" I asked her.

"Skipper," she replied, grinning. "Same as yours."

"No. Really," I insisted.

"It's Libby," she said finally. "Libby Zacks." She stared past me through the window. The bus stopped at a red light. A baby started crying in the back.

"Where are you going?" Libby asked me. "Home?"

I didn't want to tell her I had an orthodontist

appointment. That was too geeky. "I'm going to a comic book shop," I said. "The one on Goodale."

"You collect comics?" She sounded surprised. "So do I."

It was my turn to be surprised. Most of the comic book collectors I know are boys. "What kind do you collect?" I asked.

"*High School Harry & Beanhead*," she replied. "I collect all the digest-sized ones and some of the regular ones, too."

"Yuck." I made a face. "High School Harry and his pal Beanhead? Those comics stink."

"They do not!" Libby insisted.

"Those are for babies," I muttered. "They're not real comics."

"They're very well written," Libby replied. "And they're funny." She stuck her tongue out at me. "Maybe you just don't get them."

"Yeah. Maybe," I said, rolling my eyes.

I gazed out of the window. The sky had grown darker. I didn't recognize any of the shops. I saw a restaurant called Pearl's and a tiny barber's shop. Had we passed the comic book shop?

Libby folded her hands over her red backpack. "What do you collect? All that superhero junk?"

"Yeah," I told her. "My collection is worth about a thousand dollars. Maybe two thousand."

"In your dreams," she shot back. She laughed. "*High School Harry* comics never go up in value," I informed her. "Even the Number Ones are worthless. You couldn't get five dollars for your whole collection."

"Why would I want to sell them?" she argued. "I don't want to sell them. And I don't care what they're worth. I just like to read them."

"Then you're not a real collector," I said.

"Are all the boys at Franklin like you?" Libby asked.

"No. I'm the coolest one," I declared.

We both laughed.

I still couldn't decide if I liked her or not. She was pretty cute-looking. And she was funny, in a nasty sort of way.

I stopped laughing when I glanced out of the window and realized I had definitely passed my stop. I saw the bare trees of a small park I'd never seen before. The bus rumbled past it, and more unfamiliar shops came into view.

I felt a sudden stab of panic in my chest. I didn't know this neighbourhood at all.

I pushed the bell and jumped to my feet.

"What's your problem?" Libby demanded.

"My stop. I m-missed it," I stammered.

She moved her legs into the aisle so that I could squeeze past. The bus squealed to a stop. I called out goodbye and hurried through the back door.

Where am I? I asked myself, glancing around. Why did I let myself get into an argument with that girl? Why didn't I pay attention instead?

"Are you lost?" a voice asked.

I turned and saw to my surprise that Libby had followed me off the bus. "What are *you* doing here?" I blurted out.

"It's my stop," she replied. "I live two blocks down that way." She pointed.

"I have to go back," I said, turning to leave.

And as I turned, something came into view that made my breath catch in my throat.

"Ohh." I let out a startled cry and stared across the street. "But—that's *impossible!*" I exclaimed.

I was staring at a tall building on the other corner. A tall, pink stucco building with a bright green, domed roof.

I was staring at the secret headquarters of The Masked Mutant.

"Skipper—what's wrong?" Libby cried.

I couldn't answer her. I stared goggle-eyed at the building across the street. My mouth dropped open. My jaw nearly hit my knees!

I raised my eyes to the bright green roof. Then I slowly lowered them over the shiny pink walls. I had never seen colours like these in real life. They were comic book colours.

It was a comic book building.

But here it was, standing on the corner across the street.

"Skipper? Are you okay?" Libby's voice sounded far away.

It's real! I told myself. The secret headquarters building of The Masked Mutant is real!

Or *is* it?

Two hands shook me by the shoulders, snapping me out of my amazed thoughts. "Skipper! Are you in shock or something?"

"Th-that building!" I stammered.

270

"Isn't that the ugliest thing you ever saw?" Libby asked, shaking her head. She pushed back her carrot-coloured plait and hiked her backpack on to her shoulder.

"But it—it's—" I still couldn't speak.

"My dad says the architect had to be colour blind," Libby said. "It doesn't even look like a building. It looks like an airship standing on its end."

"How long has it been there?" I asked, my eyes studying the glass doors that were the only entrance.

Libby shrugged. "I don't know. My family only moved here last spring. It was already here."

The clouds darkened overhead. A cold wind swirled around the corner.

"Who do you think works in there?" Libby asked. "There's no sign or anything on the building."

Of *course* there's no sign, I thought. It's the secret headquarters of the world's most evil villain. There's no way The Masked Mutant would put a sign out the front!

He doesn't want The League of Good Guys to find his secret headquarters, I told myself.

"This is crazy," I cried.

I turned and saw Libby staring at me. "You sure you're okay? It's just a building, Skipper. No need to go ballistic."

I could feel my face turning red. Libby must think I'm some kind of a nut, I realized. "I—I think I've seen this building somewhere before," I tried to explain.

"I've got to get home," she said, glancing up at the darkening sky. "Want to come round? I'll show you my comic book collection."

"No. I'm late for my orthodontist appointment," I replied.

"Huh?" She narrowed her green eyes at me. "You said you were going to a comic book shop."

I could feel my face turning even redder. "Uh . . . I'm going to the comic book shop *after* my appointment," I told her.

"How long have you had your brace?" she asked.

I groaned. "For ever."

She started backing away. "Well, see you sometime."

"Yeah. Bye."

She turned and jogged down the street. She must think I'm a total geek, I thought unhappily.

But I couldn't help it. I really was in shock, seeing that building. I turned back to it. The top of the building had become hidden by the lowering clouds. Now the building looked like a sleek, pink rocket ship, reaching up to the clouds.

A moving truck rumbled past. I waited for it to go by, then hurried across the street.

There was no one on the pavement. I hadn't seen anyone go into the building or come out of it.

It's just a big office building, I told myself. Nothing to get excited about.

But my heart was pounding as I stopped a few feet from the glass doors at the entrance. I took a deep breath and peeked in.

I know it's crazy, but I really expected to see people wearing superhero costumes walking around in there.

I narrowed my eyes and squinted through the glass doors.

I couldn't see anyone. It appeared dark inside.

I took a step closer. Then another.

I brought my face right up to the glass and peered in. I could see a wide lobby. Pink-and-yellow walls. A row of lifts near the back.

But no people. No one. Empty.

I grabbed the glass-door handle. My throat made a loud gulping sound as I swallowed hard.

Should I go in? I asked myself. Do I dare?

My hand tightened on the glass-door handle. I started to tug the heavy door open.

Then, out of the corner of my eye, I saw a blue-and-white bus moving towards me. I glanced at my watch. I was only five minutes late for my appointment. If I jumped on the bus, I could be at the orthodontist's office in a few minutes.

Letting go of the handle, I turned and ran to the bus stop, my backpack bouncing on my shoulders. I felt disappointed. But I also felt relieved.

Walking into the headquarters of the meanest mutant in the universe was a little scary.

The bus eased to a stop. I waited for an elderly man to step off. Then I climbed on board, dropped my money into the box, and hurried to the back of the bus.

I wanted to get one last look at the mysterious pink-and-green building.

Two women were sitting in the back seat. But I pushed between them and pressed my face against the back window.

As the bus pulled away, I stared at the building. Its colours stayed bright, even though the sky was so dark behind it. The pavement was empty. I still hadn't seen anyone come out or go inside.

A few seconds later, the building disappeared into the distance. I turned away from the window and walked up the aisle to find a seat.

Weird, I thought. Totally weird.

"And it was the exact same building as in the comic book?" Wilson asked. His blue eyes stared across the lunchroom table at me.

I nodded. "As soon as I got home yesterday afternoon, I checked out the comic book. The building was exactly the same."

Wilson pulled a sandwich from his lunch bag and started to unwrap the foil. "What kind of sandwich did your mum pack for you?" he asked.

I opened mine. "Tuna salad. What's yours?"

He lifted a slice of bread and examined his sandwich. "Tuna salad," he replied. "Want to swap?"

"We both have tuna salad," I told him. "Why do you want to swap?"

He shrugged. "I don't know."

We swapped sandwiches. His mum's tuna salad was better than mine. I pulled the juice carton from my lunch bag. Then I threw the apple in the bin. I keep telling Mum not to pack an apple. I told her I just threw it away every day. Why does she keep packing one?

"Can I have your pudding container?" I asked Wilson.

"No," he replied.

I finished the first half of the sandwich. I was thinking hard about the mysterious building. I'd been thinking about it ever since I saw it.

"I've solved the mystery," Wilson said. He scratched his white-blond curls. A smile formed on his face. "Yes! I've solved it!"

"What?" I demanded eagerly.

"It's simple," Wilson replied. "Who draws The Masked Mutant?"

"The artist?" I asked. "Jimmy Starenko, of course. Starenko *created* The Masked Mutant and The League of Good Guys." How could Wilson not know that?

"Well, I'll bet this guy Starenko was here one day," Wilson continued, jabbing the straw into the top of his juice carton.

"Starenko? Here? In Riverview Falls?" I said. I wasn't following him.

Wilson nodded. "Let's say Starenko is here. He's driving down the street, and he sees the weird building. He stops his car. He gets out. He stares at the building. And he thinks: What a great building! This building would make a perfect secret headquarters building for The Masked Mutant."

"Wow. I see," I murmured. I was catching on to Wilson's thinking. "You mean, he saw the building, liked it, and copied it when he drew the headquarters building."

Wilson nodded. He had a piece of celery stuck to his front tooth. "Yeah. Maybe he got out of the car and sketched the building. Then he kept the sketches in a drawer or something till he needed them."

It made sense.

Actually, it made too much sense. I felt really disappointed. I knew it was silly, but I really *wanted* that building to be The Masked Mutant's secret headquarters.

Wilson had spoiled everything. Why did he have to be so sensible for once?

"I've got some new rubber stamps," he told me, finishing the last spoonful from his pudding container. "Want to see them? I could bring them over to your house after school."

"No thanks," I replied. "That would be *too* exciting."

I planned to take the bus and go to see the building again that afternoon. But Ms Partridge

277

gave us a ton of homework. I had to go straight home.

The next day, it snowed. Wilson and I and some other guys went tobogganing on Grover's Hill.

A week later, I finally had a chance to go back and take another look at the building. This time, I'm going inside, I told myself. There must be a receptionist or a guard, I decided. I'll ask whose building it is and who works there.

I was feeling really brave as I climbed on to the bus after school. It was an ordinary office building, after all. Nothing to get excited about.

Taking a seat at the front of the bus, I looked for Libby. The bus was filled with kids going home after school. Near the back, I saw a red-haired girl arguing with another girl. But it wasn't Libby.

No sign of her.

I stared out of the window as the bus rolled past the comic book shop. Then, a few blocks later, we bounced past my orthodontist's office. Just seeing his building made my teeth ache!

It was a sunny, clear afternoon. Bright sunlight kept filling the bus windows, forcing me to shield my eyes as I stared out.

I had to keep careful watch, because I wasn't sure where the stop was. I really didn't know this neighbourhood at all.

Kids were jammed in the aisle. So I couldn't

see out of the windows on the other side of the bus.

I hope we haven't already passed the building, I thought. I had a heavy feeling in the pit of my stomach. I have a real fear of getting lost.

My mum says that when I was two, she lost me for a few minutes in the frozen foods section at the supermarket. I think I've had a fear of getting lost ever since.

The bus pulled up to a bus stop. I recognized the small park across the street. This was the stop!

"Getting off!" I shouted, jumping into the aisle. I hit a boy with my backpack as I stumbled to the front door. "Sorry. Getting off! Getting off!"

I pushed through the crowd of kids and leaped down the steps, on to the kerb. The bus rumbled away. Sunlight streamed around me.

I stepped to the corner. Yes. This was the right stop. I recognized it all now.

I turned and raised my eyes to the strange building.

And found myself staring at a large, empty lot.

The building was gone.

"Whoa!" I cried, frozen in shock.

Shielding my eyes with one hand, I stared across the street. How could that enormous building vanish in one week?

I didn't have long to think about it. Another bus pulled up to the bus stop. "Skipper! Hey—Skipper!" Libby hopped off the bus, waving and calling my name.

She was wearing the same red-and-blue ski sweater and faded jeans, torn at one knee. Her hair was pulled straight back, tied in a ponytail with a blue hair scrunchie.

"Hey—what are you doing back in *my* neighbourhood?" she asked, smiling as she ran over to me.

"Th-that building!" I stammered, pointing to the vacant lot. "It's gone!"

Libby's expression changed. "Well, don't say hi or anything," she muttered, frowning at me.

"Hi," I said. "What happened to that building?"

She turned and followed my stare. Then she shrugged. "Guess they've knocked it down."

"But—but—" I sputtered.

"It was so ugly," Libby said. "Maybe the city *made* them knock it down."

"But did you *see* them knock it down?" I demanded impatiently. "You live near here, right? Did you see them doing it?"

She thought about it, crinkling her green eyes as she thought. "Well . . . no," she replied finally. "I've gone past here a few times, but—"

"You didn't see any machinery?" I demanded anxiously. "Any big wrecking balls? Any bulldozers? Dozens of workers?"

Libby shook her head. "No. I didn't actually see anyone knocking the building down. But I didn't really look."

She pulled her red backpack off her shoulder and held the strap in front of her with both hands. "I don't know *why* you're so interested in that ugly building, Skipper. I'm glad it's gone."

"But it was in a comic book!" I blurted out.

"Huh?" She stared hard at me. "What are you talking about?"

I knew she wouldn't understand. "Nothing," I muttered.

"Skipper, did you come all the way out here just to see that building?" she asked.

"No way," I lied. "Of course not."

"Do you want to come to my house and see my comic book collection?"

I was so frazzled and mixed up, I said yes.

I hurried out of Libby's house less than an hour later. Those *High School Harry & Beanhead* comics are the most boring comics in the world! And the art is so lame. Can't everyone see that the two girls are drawn exactly the same, except one has blonde hair and one has black?

Yuck!

Libby insisted on showing me every *High School Harry & Beanhead* comic she had. And she had shelves full of them!

Of course I couldn't concentrate on those boring comics. I couldn't stop thinking about the weird building. How could a whole building vanish without a trace?

I jogged back to the bus stop on Main Street. The sun was sinking behind the buildings. Long blue shadows tilted over the pavements.

When I get to the corner, I bet the building will be back! I found myself thinking.

But of course it wasn't.

I know. I know. I have weird thoughts. I guess it comes from reading too many comic books.

I had to wait nearly half an hour for the bus to come. I spent the whole time staring at the empty lot, thinking about the vanished building.

282

When I finally got home, I found a brown envelope waiting for me on the little table in the hall where Mum drops the mail.

"Yes!" I exclaimed happily. The special issue of *The Masked Mutant*! The comics company was sending out two special editions this month, and this was the first.

I called "hi" to my mum, tossed my coat and heavy backpack on to the floor, and raced up the stairs to my room, the comic book gripped tightly in my hot little hand.

I couldn't wait to see what had happened after The Galloping Gazelle sneaked into The Masked Mutant's headquarters. Carefully, I slid the comic book out of the envelope and examined the cover.

And there it stood. The pink-and-green headquarters building. Right on the cover.

My hand trembled as I opened to the first page. *MORNING OF A MUTANT* was the big title in scary red letters. The Masked Mutant stood in front of a big communications console.

He stared into a wall of about Twenty TV monitors. Each TV monitor showed a different member of The League of Good Guys.

"I'm tracking each one of them," The Masked Mutant said in the first dialogue balloon. "They'll never find me. I've thrown an Invisibility Curtain around my entire headquarters!"

My mouth dropped open as I read those words.

I read them three times before I let the comic book slip out of my hands to my bed.

An Invisibility Curtain.

No one can see The Masked Mutant's building because he's slipped an Invisibility Curtain around it.

I sat excitedly on the edge of my bed, breathing hard, feeling the blood pulse at my temples.

Is that what happened in real life?

Is that why I couldn't see the pink-and-green building this afternoon?

Was the comic book giving me the answer to the mystery of the missing building?

It sounded crazy. It sounded *totally* crazy.

But was it real? Was there *really* an Invisibility Curtain hiding the building?

My head was spinning faster than The Amazing Tornado-Man! I knew only one thing. I had to go back there and find out.

After school the next afternoon, I had to go with my mum to the shops to buy trainers. I usually try on at least ten or twelve pairs, then beg for the most expensive ones. You know. The ones that pump up or flash lights when you walk in them.

But this time I bought the first pair I saw, plain black-and-white Reeboks. I mean, who could think about trainers when an invisible building was waiting to be discovered?

Driving home from the shops, I started to tell Mum about the building. But she stopped me after a few sentences. "I wish you were as interested in your schoolwork as you are in those stupid comics," she said, sighing.

That's what she always says.

"When is the last time you read a good book?" she continued.

That's the *next* thing she always says.

I decided to change the subject. "We dissected

a worm today for science," I told her.

She made a disgusted face. "Doesn't your teacher have anything better to do than to cut up poor, innocent worms?"

There was just no pleasing Mum today.

The next afternoon, wearing my new trainers, I eagerly hopped on the city bus. Tossing my token into the box, I saw Libby sitting near the back. As the bus lurched away from the kerb, I stumbled down the aisle and dropped beside her, lowering my backpack to the floor.

"I'm going back to that building," I said breathlessly. "I think there's an Invisibility Curtain around it."

"Don't you ever say hi?" she complained, rolling her eyes.

I said hi. Then I repeated what I had said about the Invisibility Curtain. I told her I'd read about it in the newest *Masked Mutant* comic, and that the comic may be giving clues as to what was happening in real life.

Libby listened to me intently, not blinking, not moving. I could see that she was finally starting to see why I was so excited about finding this building.

When I finished explaining everything, she put a hand on my forehead. "You don't *feel* hot," she said. "Are you seeing a shrink?"

"Huh?" I pushed her hand away.

"Are you seeing a shrink? You're totally out of your mind. You know that—don't you?"

"I'm not crazy," I said. "I'll prove it. Come with me."

She edged closer to the window, as if trying to get away from me. "No way," she declared. "I can't believe I'm sitting here with a boy who thinks that comic books come to life."

She pointed out of the window. "Hey, look, Skipper—there goes the Easter Bunny! He's handing an egg to the Tooth Fairy!" She laughed. A mean laugh.

"Ha-ha," I muttered angrily. I have a good sense of humour. But I don't like being laughed at by girls who collect *High School Harry & Beanhead* comics.

The bus pulled up to the bus stop. I hoisted my backpack and scrambled out of the back exit. Libby stepped off right behind me.

As the bus pulled away, sending out puffs of black exhaust behind it, I gazed across the street.

No building. An empty lot.

"Well?" I turned to Libby. "You coming?"

She twisted her mouth into a thoughtful expression. "To that empty lot? Skipper, aren't you going to feel like a jerk when there's nothing there?"

"Well, go home then," I told her sharply.

"Okay. I'll come," she said, grinning.

We crossed the street. Two teenagers on bikes nearly ran us over. "Missed 'em!" one of them cried. The other one laughed.

"How do we get through the Invisibility Curtain?" Libby asked. Her voice sounded serious. But I could see by her eyes that she was laughing at me.

"In the comic book, people just stepped through it," I told her. "You can't feel it or anything. It's like a smoke screen. But once you step through it, you can see the building."

"Okay. Let's try it," Libby said. She tossed her ponytail over her shoulder. "Let's get this over with, okay?"

Walking side by side, we took a step across the pavement towards the empty lot. Then another step. Then another.

We crossed the pavement and stepped on to the hard dirt.

"I can't believe I'm doing this," Libby grumbled. We took another step. "I can't believe I'm—"

She stopped because the building popped into view.

"Ohhh!" We both cried out in unison. She grabbed my wrist and squeezed it hard. Her hand was ice-cold.

We stood a few feet from the glass entrance. The bright walls of the pink-and-green building rose above us.

"You—you were right!" Libby stammered, still squeezing my wrist.

I swallowed hard. I tried to talk, but my mouth was suddenly too dry. I coughed, and no words came out.

"Now what?" Libby asked, staring up at the shiny walls.

I still couldn't speak.

The comic book is *real*! I thought. The comic book is real.

Does that mean the building really belongs to The Masked Mutant?

Whoa! I warned myself to slow down. My heart was already racing faster than Speedboy.

"Now what?" Libby repeated impatiently. "Let's get *away* from here—okay?" For the first time, she sounded really frightened.

"No way!" I told her. "Come on. Let's go in."

She tugged me back. "Go in? Are you *crazy*?"

"We have to," I told her. "Come on. Don't stop to think about it. Let's go."

I took a deep breath, pulled open the heavy glass door, and we slipped inside.

We took one step into the brightly-lit lobby. My heart was pounding so hard, my chest hurt. My knees were shaking. I'd never been so scared in my life!

I glanced quickly all around.

The lobby was enormous. It seemed to stretch on for ever. The pink-and-yellow walls gave off a soft glow. The sparkly white ceiling seemed to be a mile above our heads.

I didn't see a reception desk. No chairs or tables. No furniture of any kind.

"Where *is* everyone?" Libby whispered. I could see that she was frightened, too. She clung to my arm, standing close beside me.

The vast room was empty. Not another person in sight.

I took another step.

And heard a soft *beep*.

A beam of yellow light shot out of the wall and rolled down over my body.

I felt a gentle tingling. Kind of a prickly feeling, the kind of feeling when your arm goes to sleep.

It swept down quickly from my head to my feet. A second or two later, the light vanished and the tingly feeling went away.

"What was *that*?" I whispered to Libby.

"What was *what*?" she replied.

"Didn't you feel that?"

She shook her head. "I didn't feel anything. Are you trying to scare me or something, Skipper?"

"It was some kind of electric beam," I told her. "It shone on me when I stepped forward."

"Let's get out of here," she muttered. "It's so quiet, it's creepy."

I turned my eyes to the row of lifts against the yellow wall. Did I dare take a ride on one? Was I brave enough to do a little exploring?

"It—it's just a big office building," I told Libby, trying to work up my courage.

"Well, if it's an office building, where are the workers?" she demanded.

"Maybe the offices are closed," I suggested.

"On a Thursday?" Libby replied. "It isn't a holiday or anything. I think the building is empty, Skipper. I don't think anyone works here."

I took a few steps towards the lifts. My trainers thudded loudly on the hard marble floor. "But all the lights are on, Libby," I said. "And the door was open."

She hurried to catch up with me. Her eyes kept darting back and forth. I could see she was really scared.

"I know what you're thinking," she said. "You don't think this is just an office building. You think this is the secret headquarters of that comic book character—don't you, Skipper?"

I swallowed hard. My knees were still shaking. I tried to make them stop, but they wouldn't.

"Well, maybe it is," I replied, staring at the lifts across from us. "I mean, how do you explain the Invisibility Curtain? It was in the comic book—and it was outside this building."

"I—I can't explain it," Libby stammered. "It's weird. It's *too* weird. This place gives me the creeps, Skipper. I really think—"

"There's only one way to find out the truth," I said. I tried to sound brave, but my voice shook nearly as much as my knees!

Libby followed my gaze to the lifts. She guessed what I was thinking. "No way!" she cried, stepping back towards the glass doors.

"We'll just ride up and down," I told her. "Maybe open the lift doors on a few floors and peek out."

"No way," Libby repeated. Her face suddenly appeared very pale. Her green eyes were wide with fright.

"Libby, it will only take a minute," I insisted. "We've come this far. I have to explore a little. I don't want to go home without finding out what this building is."

"*You* can ride the lifts," she said. "I'm going home." She backed up to the glass doors.

Outside I saw a blue-and-white bus stop at the kerb. A woman climbed off, carrying a baby in one hand, dragging a pushchair in the other.

I could run out of the door and climb right on to that bus, I thought. I could get out of here, safe and sound. And be on my way home.

But what would happen when I got home?

I would feel like a coward, a total wimp. And I would spend day after day wondering about this building, wondering if I had actually discovered the secret headquarters of a real supervillain.

If I jumped on the bus and rode home now, the building would still be a mystery. And the mystery would drive me crazy.

"Okay, Libby, you can go home if you want," I told her. "I'm going to take the lift to the top and back."

She stared at me thoughtfully. Then she rolled her eyes. "Okay, okay. I'll come with you," she murmured, shaking her head.

I was glad. I really didn't want to go alone.

"I'm only doing this because I feel sorry for you," Libby said, following me across the marble floor to the lifts.

293

"Huh? Why do you feel sorry for me?" I demanded.

"Because you're so messed up," she replied. "You really think a comic book can come to life. That's sad. That's really sad."

"Thank goodness High School Harry and Beanhead can't come to life!" I teased. Then I added, "What about the Invisibility Curtain? That was real—wasn't it?"

Libby didn't reply. Instead, she laughed. "You're serious about this!" she said. The sound of her laughter echoed in the enormous, empty lobby.

It made me feel a little braver. I laughed, too.

What's the big deal? I asked myself. So you're going to take a lift ride. So what?

It's not like The Masked Mutant is going to jump into the lift with us, I assured myself. We'll probably peek out at a lot of boring offices. And that's all.

I pushed the lighted button on the wall. Instantly, the silvery lift door in front of us slid open.

I poked my head into the lift. It had walls of dark brown wood with a silver railing that went all the way around.

There were no signs on the walls. No building directory. No words at all.

I suddenly realized there were no signs in the lobby, either. Not even a sign with the name of the building. Or a sign to tell visitors where to check in.

Weird.

"Let's go," I said.

Libby held back. I tugged her by the arm into the lift.

The doors slid shut silently behind us as soon as we stepped in. I turned to the control panel to the left of the door. It was a long, silvery rectangle filled with buttons.

I pushed the button to the top floor.

The lift started to hum. It jerked slightly as we began to move.

I turned to Libby. She had her back pressed against the wall, her hands shoved into her jeans pockets. She stared straight ahead at the door.

"We're moving," I murmured.

The lift picked up speed.

"Hey!" Libby and I both cried out at the same time.

"We—we're going *down*!" I exclaimed.

I had pushed the button to the top floor. But we were dropping. Fast.

Faster.

I grabbed the railing with both hands.

Where was it taking us?

Would it ever stop?

The lift stopped with a hard *thud* that made my knees bend. "Whoa!" I cried.

I let go of the railing and turned to Libby beside me. "You okay?"

She nodded. She stared straight ahead at the lift door.

"We should have gone up," I muttered tensely. "I pushed *up*."

"Why doesn't the door open?" Libby asked in a trembling voice.

We both stared at the door. I stepped to the centre of the lift. "Open!" I commanded it.

The door didn't move.

"We're trapped in here," Libby said, her voice getting shrill and tiny.

"No," I replied, still trying to be the brave one. "It'll open. Watch. It's just slow."

The door didn't open.

"The lift must be broken," Libby wailed. "We'll be trapped down here for ever. The air is starting to run out already. I can't breathe!"

"Don't panic," I warned, struggling to keep my voice calm. "Take a deep breath, Libby. There's plenty of air."

She obediently sucked in a deep breath. She let it out in a long *whoosh.* "Why won't the door open? I *knew* we shouldn't have done this!"

I turned to the control panel. A button at the bottom read OPEN. I pushed it. Instantly, the door slid open.

I turned back to Libby. "See? We're okay."

"But where *are* we?" she cried.

I stepped to the doorway and poked my head out. It was very dark. I could see some kind of heavy machinery in the darkness.

"We're in the basement, I think," I told Libby. "There are all kinds of pipes and a big boiler and things."

"Let's go," Libby urged, hanging back against the wall of the lift.

I took a step out of the door and glanced both ways. I couldn't see much. More machinery. A row of metal bins. A stack of long metal boxes.

"Come on, Skipper," Libby demanded. "Let's go back up. Now!"

I stepped back into the elevator and pushed the button marked LOBBY.

The door didn't close. The lift didn't move, didn't hum.

I pushed LOBBY again. I pushed it five or six times.

Nothing happened.

I suddenly had a lump in my throat as big as a watermelon. I really didn't want to be stuck down in this dark basement.

I started pushing buttons wildly. I pushed everything. I pushed a red button marked EMERGENCY five or six times.

Nothing.

"I don't *believe* this!" I choked out.

"Let's get out and take a different lift," Libby suggested.

Good idea, I thought. There was a long row of lifts up in the lobby. We'll just get out of this one and push the button for another one to come down and get us.

I led the way out into the dark basement. Libby stayed close behind me.

"Oh!" We both let out low cries as the lift door quickly slid shut behind us.

"What's going on?" I demanded. "Why wouldn't it close before?"

Libby didn't reply.

I waited for my eyes to adjust to the darkness. Then I saw what Libby was staring at.

"Where are the other lifts?" she cried.

We were staring at a smooth, bare wall. The lift that had brought us down here was the only lift on the wall.

I spun around, checking out the other walls. But it was too dark to see very far.

"The other lifts don't come down here, I guess," Libby murmured in a trembling voice.

I searched the wall for a button to push to bring our lift back. I couldn't find one. No button.

"There's no way out!" Libby wailed. "No way out at all!"

"Maybe there are lifts on the other wall," I said, pointing across the huge, dark room.

"Maybe," Libby repeated doubtfully.

"Maybe there's a staircase or something," I said.

"Maybe," she said softly.

A sudden noise made me jump. A rumble followed by a grinding hum.

"Just the boiler starting up," I told Libby.

"Let's find a way out of here," she urged. "I'm never going in a lift again as long as I live!"

I could feel her hand on my shoulder as I started to make my way through the darkness. The huge, grey boiler rumbled and coughed. Another big machine made a soft clattering sound as we edged past it.

"Anybody down here?" I called. My voice echoed off the long, dust-covered pipes that ran along the low ceiling above our heads. I cupped

300

my hands around my mouth and called again. "Anybody here? Can anybody hear me?"

Silence.

The only sounds I could hear were the rumble of the boiler and the soft scrape of our trainers as Libby and I slowly crept over the floor.

As we came near the far wall, we could see that there were no lifts over here. The smooth plaster wall was bare except for a thick tangle of cobwebs up near the ceiling.

"There's *got* to be some stairs leading out of here," Libby whispered, close behind me.

Dim light shone through a narrow doorway up ahead. "Let's see where this leads," I said, brushing stringy spiderwebs off my face.

We stepped through the doorway and found ourselves in a long hallway. Dust-covered ceiling bulbs cast pale light on to the concrete floor.

"Anybody here?" I called again. My voice sounded hollow in the long tunnel of a hallway.

No reply.

Dark doorways lined both sides of the hallway. I peeked into each door as we passed. I saw stacks of boxes, tall filing cabinets, strange machinery I didn't recognize. One large room was jammed with enormous coils of metal cable. Another room had sheets of metal piled nearly to the ceiling.

"Helloooooo!" I called. "Hellllooooooo!"

No reply.

Flashing red lights inside a large room caught my eye. I stopped at the doorway and stared in at some sort of control panel.

One wall was filled with blinking red and green lights. In front of the lights stood a long counter of dials and gears and levers. Three tall stools were placed along the counter. But no one was sitting in them.

No one was working the controls. The room was empty. As empty as the rest of this strange, frightening basement.

"Weird, huh?" I whispered to Libby.

When she didn't answer, I turned to make sure she was okay.

"Libby?"

She was gone.

I spun around. "Libby?"

My entire body shook.

"Where are you?"

I squinted back down the long, grey hallway. No sign of her.

"Libby? If this is some kind of a stupid joke..." I started. But the rest of my words caught in my throat.

Breathing hard, I forced myself to retrace our steps. "Libby?" I stopped at every door and called her name. "Libby?"

The hallway curved, and I followed it. I began jogging, my hands down stiffly at my sides, calling her name, searching every door, peering into every dark room.

How could she get lost? I asked myself, feeling my panic rise until I could barely breathe. She was right behind me.

I turned another corner. Into a hallway I hadn't explored yet. "Libby?"

The narrow hall led to an enormous, brightly-lit room. I had to shut my eyes against the sudden bright light.

When I opened them, I found myself nearly face-to-face with a gigantic machine. Bright floodlights from the high ceiling covered it in light.

The machine had to be a block long! A big control panel, filled with dials, and buttons, and lights, stood against the side. A long, flat part—like a conveyor belt—led to several rollers. And at the very end of the machine stood a huge white wheel. No—a cylinder. No—a roll of white paper.

It's a printing press! I realized.

I lurched into the room, stepping around stacks of paper and cardboard boxes. The floor was littered with paper, ink-smeared paper, crumpled, folded, and ripped.

As I staggered towards the huge printing press, the sea of paper rose up nearly to my knees!

"Libby? Are you in here? Libby?"

Silence.

This room was as empty as all the others.

The paper crackled under my trainers. I made my way to a long table at the back of the room. I found a red stool in front of the table, and I dropped down on it.

I kicked big sheets of paper away from my legs

and glanced around the room. A hundred questions pushed into my mind at once.

Where is Libby? How could she disappear like that?

Is she somewhere close behind me? Will she follow the hallway to this big room?

Where is everyone? Why is this place totally deserted?

Is this where they print the comic books? Am I in the basement of Collectable Comics, the company that publishes *The Masked Mutant*?

Questions, questions.

My brain felt about to burst. I stared around the cluttered room, my eyes rolling past the gigantic printing press, searching for Libby.

Where was she? *Where?*

I turned back to the table—and gasped.

I nearly toppled off the stool. The Masked Mutant was staring up at me.

A large, colour drawing of The Masked Mutant stared at me from the table. Startled, I picked it up and examined it.

It had been drawn on thick posterboard in coloured inks. The Masked Mutant's cape swept behind him. Through his mask, his eyes appeared to stare out at me. Evil, angry eyes.

The ink glistened on the page, as if still wet. I rubbed my thumb over an edge of the cape. The ink didn't come off.

I wonder if Starenko drew this portrait, I thought, studying it.

Glancing across the table, I saw a stack of papers on a low counter that ran along the entire back wall. Hopping off the tall stool, I made my way over to the counter and began shuffling through the papers.

They were ink drawings and pencil sketches. Many of them were of The Masked Mutant. They showed him in different poses. Some of them showed him moving his molecules around, changing into wild animals and strange, unearthly creatures.

I opened a thick folder and found about a dozen colour sketches of the members of The League of Good Guys. Then I found a stack of pencil drawings of characters I'd never seen before.

This *must* be where they make the comic books! I told myself.

I was so excited about seeing these actual drawings and sketches, I nearly forgot about Libby.

This pink-and-green building must be the headquarters of Collectable Comics, I realized.

I was starting to feel calmer. My fears dropped away like feathers off The Battling Bird-Boy.

After all, there was nothing to be afraid of. I hadn't stumbled into the headquarters of the world's most evil supervillain. I was in the basement of the comic book offices.

This is where the writers and artists worked. And this is where they print the comic books every month.

So why should I be afraid?

I shuffled through folder after folder, making my way down the long counter. I found a pile of layouts for a comic book that I had just bought.

It was so exciting seeing the actual art. The page was really big, at least twice as big as the comic book. I guessed that the artists made their drawings much bigger than the actual page. And then they shrank the drawings down when they printed them.

I found some really new pencil drawings of The Masked Mutant. I knew they were new because I didn't recognize them from my comics at home—and I have them all!

Drawing after drawing. My eyes were practically spinning!

I never dreamed that Collectable Comics were made right in Riverview Falls.

I flipped through a sketchbook of Penguin People portraits. I never liked the Penguin People. I know they're good guys, and people really think they're great. But I think their black-and-white costumes just look silly.

I was having a great time. Really enjoying myself.

Of course it had to end.

It ended when I opened the last folder on the counter. And stared at the sketches inside.

I gaped at them in disbelief, my hands trembling as I shuffled down from one to the next.

"This is impossible!" I cried out loud.

I was staring at sketches of ME.

15

I frantically shuffled through the big stack of drawings.

You're just imagining it, Skipper, I told myself. The boy in the sketches only looks like you. It isn't really you.

But it *had* to be me.

In every drawing, the boy had my round face, my dark hair—cut short on the sides and long on top.

He was short like me. And just a little bit chubby. He had my crooked smile, up a little higher on one side. He wore my clothes—baggy jeans and long-sleeved, pocket T-shirts.

I stopped at a drawing halfway through the pile and stared hard at it, holding it close to my face. "Oh, wow!" I exclaimed.

The boy in the drawing even had a chip in his front tooth. Just like me.

"It's impossible!" I cried out loud, my voice tiny and shrill in the enormous room.

Who had been drawing me? And why? Why would a comic book artist make sketch after sketch of me?

And how did the artist know me so well? How did the artist know that I have a tiny chip in one front tooth?

A cold shiver ran down my back. I suddenly felt very frightened. I stared at the drawings, my heart pounding.

In one drawing, I looked really scared. I was running from something, my arms out stiffly in front of me.

Another drawing was a close-up portrait of my face. My expression in the sketch was angry. No. More than angry. I looked furious.

Another sketch showed me flexing my muscles. Hey, I look pretty cool! I thought. The artist had given me bulging superhero biceps.

In another drawing, my eyes were closed. Was I asleep? Or was I dead?

I was still staring at the drawings, shuffling from one to the next, studying each one—when I heard the footsteps.

And realized I was no longer alone.

"Who-who's there?" I cried, whirling around.

"Where *were* you?" Libby demanded angrily, running across the room towards me. "I searched everywhere!"

"Where were *you*?" I shot back. "I thought you were right behind me."

"I thought you were right *ahead* of me!" she cried. "I turned a corner, and you were gone." She stopped in front of me, breathing hard, her face bright red. "How could you leave me by myself in this creepy place?"

"I didn't!" I insisted. "You left *me*!"

She shook her head, still gasping for breath. "Well, let's get *out* of here, Skipper. I've found some lifts that are working." She tugged my sleeve.

I picked up the stack of drawings. "Look, Libby." I held them up to her. "You have to see these."

"Are you serious?" she cried. "I want to get *out*

of here. I don't want to look at comic book drawings now!"

"But—but—" I sputtered, waving the drawings.

She turned and started towards the doorway. "I *told* you I've found some lifts. Are you coming or not?"

"But these are drawings of *me*!" I cried.

"Yeah. Sure," she called back sarcastically. She stopped at the front of the big printing press and turned back to me. "Why would anyone draw *you*, Skipper?"

"I-I don't know," I stammered. "But these drawings—"

"You have a sick imagination," she said. "You seem like a normal guy. But you're totally weird. Bye." Libby started jogging over the paper-cluttered floor to the door.

"No—wait!" I called. I dropped the drawings on to the counter, slid off the tall stool, and chased after her. "Wait up, Libby!"

I followed her out into the hall. I didn't want to be left alone in this creepy place, either. I had to get home and think about this. I had to puzzle it out.

My head was spinning. I felt totally confused.

I followed her through the long tunnel of hallways. We turned a corner, and I saw a row of lifts against the wall.

Libby pushed the button on the wall, and one

of the lifts slid open silently. We both peered carefully inside before stepping in. It was empty.

We were both panting. My head was throbbing. My side ached. Neither of us spoke a word.

Libby pushed the button marked LOBBY. We heard a soft hum and felt the lift start to move.

When the door slid open, and we saw the pink-and-yellow walls of the lobby, Libby and I both cheered. We burst out of the lift together and ran across the marble floor to the exit.

Out on the pavement, I stopped, lowering my hands to my knees, sucking in deep breaths of fresh air. When I glanced up, I saw Libby studying her watch.

"I've got to get home," she said. "My mum is going to have a cow!"

"Do you believe me about the drawings?" I asked breathlessly.

"No," she replied. "Who would believe *that*?" She waved and made her way across the street, heading for home.

I could see a bus approaching, a few blocks down. Searching in my jeans pocket for some change, I turned to take one last look at the weird building.

It had vanished once again.

I needed time to think about everything that had happened. But Wilson was waiting for me when

I got home, and he followed me up to my room.

"I brought over some of my rubber stamps," he said, raising a brown paper bag up to my face. He turned it over and emptied it on to my desk. "I thought you might like to see some of the better ones."

"Wilson—" I started. "I really don't—"

"This one is a ladybird," he said, holding up a small wooden stamp. "It's very old. It's the oldest one I own. Here. I'll show it to you." He opened a blue inkpad, stamped the ladybird on it, and pressed it on to the top of a pad of paper I had on the desk.

"How old is it?" I asked him.

"I don't know," he replied. He held up another one. "It's a cow," he said. As if I couldn't tell. He stamped it on to the pad. "I have several cows," Wilson said. "But I only brought one."

I studied the cow, pretending to be interested.

"It's another really old one," Wilson said proudly.

"How old?" I asked.

He shrugged. "Beats me." He reached for another stamp.

"Uh . . . Wilson . . . I just had a really weird thing happen," I told him. "And I need to think about it. Alone."

He narrowed his blue eyes at me, confused. "What happened?"

"It's a bit of a long story," I said. "I was in a

building. On the north side of town. I think it's where they make the Collectable Comics."

"Really? Here in Riverview Falls?" Wilson's face filled with surprise. "And they let you in?"

"There was no one there," I told him. It felt good to share the story with someone. "So we went in. This girl I met on the bus. Libby. And me. We tried to go up in the lift. But it took us down. Then Libby got lost. And I found a stack of drawings of myself."

"Whoa!" Wilson exclaimed, raising a hand for me to stop. "I'm not following this too well, Skipper."

I realized what I had said didn't make any sense at all. How could I explain it?

I told Wilson I'd talk to him later, after I'd calmed down. I helped him gather up his rubber stamps. He'd brought about twenty of them. "Twenty of the best," he said.

I walked him downstairs and said I'd call him after dinner.

After he left, something caught my eye on the mail table in the hall. A brown envelope.

My heart jumped. Was it—? Yes! An envelope from the Collectable Comics company. The next special issue of *The Masked Mutant*.

I was so excited, I nearly knocked the whole table over as I grabbed for the envelope. I tucked it under my arm without opening it and ran up the stairs, two at a time.

I need total privacy. I have to study this! I told myself.

I closed the bedroom door behind me and dropped down on to the edge of the bed. My hands trembled as I ripped open the envelope and pulled out the comic book.

The cover showed a close-up of The Masked Mutant. His eyes glared angrily out at the reader. *A NEW FOE FOR THE MUTANT!* proclaimed the title.

Huh? A new foe?

I took a deep breath and held it. Calm down, Skipper, I urged myself. It's only a comic book.

But would this new issue help to solve the mystery for me?

Would it tell me anything about the strange, pink-and-green headquarters building? Would it help solve any of the puzzles from this afternoon?

I turned to the first page. It showed the headquarters building from above. The next drawing showed the building at street level. In the deep shadows, someone was approaching the glass doors.

Someone was sneaking into the headquarters building.

I turned the page.

And shrieked at the top of my lungs: "I don't *believe* it!"

Yes. You probably guessed it. It was *ME* sneaking into The Masked Mutant's headquarters building.

I stared at the page so hard, I thought my eyes were going to pop out of my head.

I was so excited—and so shocked—I couldn't read the words. They became a grey blur.

I turned the pages with shaking hands. I don't think I took a breath. I studied each picture, holding the comic book about an inch from my face.

The Galloping Gazelle sat in a tiny room. The room grew hotter and hotter. In minutes, The Galloping Gazelle would become The Boiled Gazelle!

The Masked Mutant had trapped The Galloping Gazelle in his headquarters. And now he planned to leave The Gazelle there to boil.

I turned the page. My hand shook so hard, I nearly tore the page off.

There I was, creeping through the dark hallway. In the comic, I wore the same T-shirt and baggy jeans I had on right now.

The next drawing showed a close-up of my face. Big balls of sweat rolled down my pink face. I guess that meant I was scared.

I'm a little too chubby in that drawing, I thought.

But it was me. It was definitely ME!

"Mum!" I screamed, closing the comic and jumping off the bed. "Mum! Dad! You have to see this!"

I tore out of my room and hurtled down the stairs. I don't think my feet touched the floor!

"Mum! Dad! Where are you?"

I found them in the kitchen, preparing dinner. Dad was chopping onions by the sink. His eyes were filled with tears. Mum was bent over the stove. As usual, she was having trouble getting the oven lit.

"I'm in this comic book!" I cried, bursting into the room.

"Not now!" they both replied in unison.

"No. You have to see this!" I insisted, waving it in front of Dad.

Dad didn't stop chopping. "You had a letter to the editor published?" he asked through his tears.

"No! I'm *in* the comic!" I told him breathlessly. I waved it closer to him.

318

"I can't see a thing!" Dad exclaimed. "Get that away from me. Can't you see what this onion is doing to my eyes?"

"There's a trick to chopping onions," Mum said, bent over the stove. "But I don't know what it is."

I ran over to Mum. "You *have* to check this out, Mum. I'm in here. Look. It's really me!"

Mum shook her head, frowning. "I can't get it to light," she said, sighing. "I think the pilot is out again."

"I'll check it if I ever stop crying," Dad told her.

"*Will you look at this?!*" I screamed, totally losing it.

Mum gave a quick glance to the page I was holding in front of her. "Yes, yes. That *does* look a little like you, Skipper," she said, waving me away. She turned back to the oven. "We really need a new stove, dear."

"Dad—take a look," I pleaded.

I ran back to him, but he had shoved a towel up to his face and was crying into the towel. "I guess you can't look now, huh?" I said softly.

He didn't answer. He just cried into the towel.

I let out a long, exasperated moan. What was their problem, anyway?

This was the most exciting thing that had ever happened to me. And they couldn't be bothered to take one look.

Angrily, I closed the comic and stomped out of the room.

"Skipper, lay the table," Mum shouted after me.

Lay the table? I'm starring in a famous comic book, and she's asking me to lay the table?

"Why can't Mitzi do it?" I asked.

"Lay the table, Skipper," Mum repeated sternly.

"Okay, okay. In a few minutes," I called back. I dropped down on to the living-room couch and turned to the back of the comic. I had been too excited to read it to the end. Now I wanted to read the part where it tells you what to expect in the next comic book.

My eyes swept over the page. There was The Galloping Gazelle, still trapped in the boiling hot room. And there stood The Masked Mutant outside the door, about to declare his victory.

I squinted at the white thought balloon over The Galloping Gazelle's head. What was he saying?

"Only the boy can save me now," The Galloping Gazelle was thinking. "Only the boy can save the world from The Masked Mutant's evil. But where is he?"

I read it again. And again.

Was it true? Was I the only one who could save The Galloping Gazelle?

Did I really have to go back there?

After school the next day, I hurried to the bus stop. It was a clear, cold day. The ground beneath my trainers was frozen hard. The sky above looked like a broad sheet of cold, blue ice.

Leaning into the sharp wind, I wondered if Libby would be on the bus. I was dying to tell her about the comic book. I wanted to tell her I was going back into the strange building.

Would she go back with me?

No way, I decided. Libby had been frightened after our first visit. I could never drag her back there.

I jogged past the playground, my eyes on the street, watching for a bus.

"Hey, Skipper!" a familiar voice called. I turned to see Wilson running after me, his coat unzipped and flapping up behind him like wings. "Skipper—what's up? You going home?"

Two blocks up, the blue-and-white bus turned the corner.

"No. I'm going somewhere," I told Wilson. "I can't look at your rubber stamp collection now."

His expression turned serious. "I'm not collecting rubber stamps any more," he said. "I've given it up."

I couldn't hide my surprise. "Huh? How come?"

"They took up too much of my time," he replied.

The bus pulled to the kerb. The door opened. "See you later," I told Wilson.

As I stepped on to the bus, I remembered where I was going. And I suddenly wondered if I *would* see Wilson later. I wondered if I would ever see him again!

Libby wasn't on the bus. In a way, I was glad. It meant I wouldn't have to explain to her what I was doing.

She would have laughed at me for believing what I read in a comic book.

But the comic book had told the truth about the Invisibility Curtain. And now it had said that I was the only one who could save The Galloping Gazelle and stop The Masked Mutant's evil.

"But it's just a comic book!" Libby would have said. "How can you be such a jerk to believe a comic book?"

That's what she would have said. And I don't

know *how* I could have answered.

So I was glad she wasn't on the bus.

I climbed off the bus in front of the empty lot. I gazed at it from across the street. I knew it wasn't really an empty lot. I knew the pink-and-green building was there, hidden behind the Invisibility Curtain.

As I crossed the street, I felt a wave of fear sweep down over me. My mouth suddenly got dry. I tried to swallow, but nearly choked. My throat felt as if someone had tied a knot in it. My stomach felt kind of fluttery. And my knees got sweaty and refused to bend.

I stopped on the pavement and struggled to calm myself down.

It's just a comic book. Just a comic book. That's what I told myself, repeating the words over and over.

Finally, staring straight ahead at the empty lot, I worked up my courage enough to move forward. One step. Another. Another.

Suddenly, the building popped into view.

I gasped. Even though I had crossed through the Invisibility Curtain before, it was still amazing to see a building suddenly appear before my eyes.

Swallowing hard, I pulled open one of the glass entrance doors and stepped into the bright, pink-and-yellow lobby.

Staying near the door, I turned to the left, then the right.

Still empty. Not a person in sight.

I coughed. My cough sounded tiny in the huge lobby. My trainers squeaked over the marble floor as I started to the lifts on the far wall.

Where *is* everyone? I asked myself. It's the middle of the afternoon. How can I be the only one in this huge lobby?

I stopped in front of the lifts. I raised my finger to the lift button—but I didn't push it.

I wish Libby *had* come along, I decided. If Libby were here, at least I'd have someone to be terrified *with*!

I pushed the lift button.

"Well . . . here goes," I murmured, waiting for the door to open.

And then someone laughed. A cold, evil laugh.

Right behind me.

I let out a low cry and spun around.

No one there.

The laughter repeated. Soft, but cruel.

My eyes darted around the lobby. I couldn't see anyone.

"Wh-who's there?" I choked out.

The laughter stopped.

I continued to search. My eyes went up to the wall above the lift. A small, black loudspeaker poked out from the yellow wall.

The laughter must have come from there, I decided. I stared up at it as if I expected to see someone in there.

Get out of here! a voice inside me begged. My sensible voice. *Just turn around, Skipper, and run out of this building as fast as your rubbery, shaky legs will take you!*

I ignored it and pressed the lift button. The lift door on the left slid open silently, and I stepped inside.

The door closed. I stared at the control panel. Should I push up or down?

The last visit, I had pushed up, the top floor—and the lift had taken Libby and me down to the basement.

My finger hesitated in front of the buttons. What would happen if this time I pushed *down*?

I didn't get a chance to find out. The lift started with a jolt before I pushed any button at all.

I grabbed on to the railing. My hand was cold and wet. The lift hummed as it rose.

I'm going up, I realized. Up to where?

The ride seemed to take for ever. I watched the floor numbers whir by on top of the control panel. Forty... forty-one... forty-two... The lift beeped each time it passed a floor.

It came to a stop at forty-six. Was this the top floor?

The door slid open. I let go of the railing and stepped out.

I glanced down a long, grey hallway. I blinked once. Twice. It looked as if I had stepped into a black-and-white movie. The walls were grey. The ceiling was grey. The floor was grey. The doors on both sides of the hall were grey.

It feels like I'm standing in a thick, grey fog, I thought, peering one way, then the other. Or in a dark cloud.

No one in sight. Nothing moving.

I listened hard. Listened for voices, for laughter, for the click and hum of office machinery.

Silence—except for the thudding of my heart.

I shoved my cold, clammy hands into the pockets of my jeans and began to walk, slowly following the hallway.

I turned a corner and stared down another endless, grey hallway. The end of the hall seemed to fade away, to fade into a grey blur.

I suddenly remembered the drawings in the newest issue of *The Masked Mutant*. A big, two-page drawing had shown the long hallways of The Masked Mutant's secret headquarters.

The long, twisting hallway in the comic book looked just like this hallway—except that the comic book hallway had bright green walls and a yellow ceiling. And the rooms were filled with costumed supervillains who worked for The Masked Mutant.

As I slowly made my way through this grey, empty hallway, I had a weird thought. Everything looked so grey and washed out, I had the feeling that I was in a sketch of a hallway. A black-and-white pencil drawing that hadn't been filled in yet.

But, of course, that didn't make any sense at all.

You're just thinking crazy thoughts because you're so scared, I told myself.

And then I heard a noise.

A hard, thumping sound. A bump.

"Whoa!" I whispered. My heart leaped up to my throat. I stopped in the middle of the hall. And listened.

Bump. Thump.

Coming from up ahead. From around the next corner?

I forced myself to walk. I turned the corner. And gasped at the bright colours.

The walls down *this* hallway were bright green. The ceiling was yellow. The thick carpet under my sneakers was a dark, wine-red.

Bump. Bump. Thump.

The colours were so bright, I had to shield my eyes with one hand.

I squinted to the end of the hall. The green walls led to a closed yellow door. The door had a metal bolt against the front.

Thump. Thump.

The sounds were coming from behind the bolted doorway.

I made my way slowly down the hall to the doorway.

I stopped outside the bolted door. "Anyone in there?" I tried to call into the room. But my voice came out in a choked whisper.

I coughed and tried again. "Anyone in there?"

No reply.

Then, another loud bumping sound. Like wood thumping against wood.

"Anyone in there?" I called, my voice a little stronger.

The thumping sounds stopped. "Can you help me?" a man's voice called from inside the room.

I froze.

"Can you help me?" the man pleaded.

I hesitated for a second. Should I try to help him?

Yes.

I raised both hands to the metal bolt. I took a deep breath and shoved the bolt with all my strength.

To my surprise, it slid easily.

The door was unlocked. I turned the handle and pushed the door open.

I stumbled off-balance into the room and stared in amazement at the figure staring back at me.

"You—you're *real*?" I cried.

His cape was twisted, and his mask had rolled down over one eye. But I knew I was staring at The Galloping Gazelle.

"You're really *alive*?" I blurted out.

"Of course," he replied impatiently. "Untie me, kid." He gazed towards the open door. "You'd better hurry."

I realized that his powerful arms and legs were tied to the chair. The thumping and bumping had been the sounds of his chair banging against the floor as he tried to escape.

"I—I can't believe that you're here!" I cried. I was so amazed—and so frightened—I didn't know what I was saying!

"I'll give you my autograph later," he said, his eyes still on the doorway. "Just hurry, okay? We've got to get out of here. I don't think we have much time."

"T-time?" I stammered.

"He'll be back," The Galloping Gazelle

330

murmured. "We want to get to him before he gets to *us*, right, kid?"

"Us??" I cried.

"Just untie me," The Galloping Gazelle instructed. "I can handle him." He shook his head. "I wish I could contact my buddies at the League. They're probably all searching the universe for me."

Still half dazed, I stumbled across the tiny room to the chair and began working at the ropes. The knots were big and tight and hard to untie. The coarse rope scraped my hands as I struggled to loosen them.

"Hurry, kid," The Galloping Gazelle urged. "Hey, how did you find the secret headquarters, anyway?"

"I . . . just found it," I replied, tugging at the knots.

"Don't be modest, kid," the superhero said in his flat, low voice. "You used your secret cyber-radar powers, right? Or did you use ultra-mind control to read my thoughts and hurry to my rescue?"

"No. I just took the bus," I replied.

I didn't really know how to answer him. Did he have me confused with someone else?

Why was I here? What was going to happen to us? To *me*?

Questions, questions. They flew through my mind as I frantically worked at the heavy ropes.

I tried to ignore the pain from the cuts and scrapes to my hands. But it hurt a lot.

Finally, one of the knots slid open. The Galloping Gazelle flexed his muscles and stretched out his powerful chest—and the ropes popped away easily.

"Thanks, kid," he boomed, jumping to his feet. He adjusted his mask so that he could see through both eyeholes. Then he swept his long cape behind him and straightened his tights.

"Okay. Let's go pay him a surprise visit," he said, pulling up the ends of his gloves. He started towards the door, taking long, heavy strides. His boots thundered loudly as he walked.

"Uh . . . do you really want *me* to come, too?" I asked, lingering behind the chair.

He nodded. "I know what you're worried about, kid. You're worried that you won't be able to keep up with me because I have dyno-legs and I'm the fastest living mutant in the known universe."

"Well . . ." I hesitated.

"Don't worry," he replied. "I'll go slow." He motioned impatiently. "Let's get moving."

I tripped over the tangle of ropes on the floor. Grabbed the chair to catch my balance. Then followed him out into the green-and-yellow hallway.

He turned and began running down the hall.

As I started to follow, he became a blue-and-red blur of light—and then vanished.

A few seconds later, he came jogging back. "Sorry. Too fast for you?" he called.

I nodded. "A little."

He rested a gloved hand heavily on my shoulder. His grey eyes peered at me solemnly through the slits in his mask. "Do you have wall-climbing abilities?" he demanded.

I shook my head. "No. Sorry."

"Okay. We'll take the stairs," he said.

He grabbed my hand and pulled me down the hall. He moved so fast, both of my feet were in the air.

I guess it was impossible for him to go slow.

The walls whirred past in a bright green blur. He pulled me around a corner, then another corner.

I felt as if I were flying! We were moving so fast, I didn't have time to breathe.

Around another corner. Then through an open doorway.

The doorway led to a flight of steep, dark stairs. I peered up to the top, but I could see only heavy blackness.

I expected The Galloping Gazelle to pull me up the stairs. But to my surprise, he stopped just past the doorway.

He narrowed his eyes at the stairs. "There is a

disintegrator-ray there," he announced, rubbing his square jaw thoughtfully.

"A *what*?" I cried.

"A disintegrator-ray," he repeated, his eyes locked on the stairs. "If you step into it, it will disintegrate you in one hundredth of a second."

I swallowed hard. My entire body started to tremble.

"Do you think you can jump the first two steps?" The Galloping Gazelle asked.

"You mean—?" I started.

"Land on the third step," he instructed. "Get a good running start."

I'll need it, I thought, staring at the steep steps.

I suddenly wished I hadn't eaten so many Pop-Tarts and bowls of Frosted Flakes for breakfast every morning. If only I were a little slimmer, a little lighter.

"Get a good running start and make sure you clear the first two steps," The Galloping Gazelle warned. "Land on the third step and keep moving. If you land on the first or second step, you'll disintegrate." He motioned with his fingers. "Poof."

I let out a low, frightened moan. I couldn't help myself. I wanted to be brave. But my body wasn't cooperating. It was shaking and quaking as if I were made of jelly.

"I'll go first," the superhero said. He turned to

the stairs, bent his knees, stretched both hands forward—and leaped over the invisible disintegrator-ray. He landed on the fifth step.

He turned around and motioned for me to follow. "See? It's easy," he said brightly.

Easy for you! I thought darkly. *Some of us don't have dyno-legs.*

"Hurry," he urged. "If you stop to think about it, you won't be able to do it."

I'm *already* thinking about it! I thought.

How can I *not* think about it?

"I—I'm not very athletic," I murmured in a tiny, trembling voice. What an understatement! Whenever the kids I know play any sports, I am always the *last* kid chosen for a team.

"Hurry," The Galloping Gazelle urged. He reached out both hands. "Take a good running jump, kid. Aim for the third step. It isn't that high. I'll catch you."

The third step looked about a mile in the air to me. But I held my breath, bent my knees, took a running leap—my *best* leap—

—and I landed with a hard *thud* on the first step.

I screamed and clamped my eyes shut as the disintegrator-ray poured through me, and my body crumbled into thin air.

Actually, I didn't feel anything.

I opened my eyes to find myself still standing on the bottom step. Still in one chubby piece.

"I—I—I—" I stammered.

"I guess he doesn't have it turned on," The Galloping Gazelle said calmly. He smiled at me through the mask. "You had a lucky escape, kid."

I was still trembling. Cold beads of sweat rolled down my forehead. I couldn't speak.

"Hope your luck holds out," The Galloping Gazelle muttered. He turned and started up the stairs, his cape floating behind him. "Come on. Let's go meet our destiny."

I didn't like the sound of that. Not one bit.

But I didn't like anything that was going on. The Galloping Gazelle had said that I was lucky.

But I certainly didn't feel lucky as I followed him up the dark stairs.

At the top landing, he pushed open a wide metal door, and we stepped into an amazing room.

The room glowed with colour. It was decorated like an office, the fanciest, most luxurious office I have ever seen.

The shaggy white carpet was soft and so thick, I sank in it nearly to my ankles. Silky blue curtains were draped over enormous windows that overlooked the town. Sparkly crystal chandeliers hung from the ceiling.

Velvety couches and chairs were arranged around dark wood tables. One wall was covered with floor-to-ceiling bookshelves, each shelf filled with leather-covered books.

A giant TV screen—dark—stood in one corner. Beside it, a wall of electronic equipment. Enormous oil paintings of green farm fields covered one wall.

A shiny, gold-plated desk stood in the middle of the room. The tall desk chair behind it looked more like a throne than a chair.

"Wow!" I cried, lingering near the door, my eyes taking in the splendour of the vast room.

"He treats himself well," The Galloping Gazelle commented. "But his time is over."

"You mean—?" I started.

"I'm too fast for him," the superhero boasted.

337

"I'll run circles around him, faster and faster—until I become a raging tornado. He'll be swept away for ever."

"Wow," I repeated. I didn't know what else to say.

"He caught me napping before," The Galloping Gazelle continued. "That's the only way he can catch me. When I'm asleep. Otherwise, I'm much too fast for him. Too fast for anybody. Know how fast I run the one-hundred metres?"

"How fast?" I asked.

"I run it in one-tenth. One-tenth of a second. That would be an Olympic record. But they don't let me in the Olympics because I'm a mutant."

I started to follow The Galloping Gazelle to the centre of the room. But I stopped when I heard the laughter.

The same cold laughter I had heard in the lobby.

I froze in fright.

And stared as the gold desk began to move. And change.

The shiny gold shimmered as it shifted and bent, raising itself up and forming a human figure.

I took a step back, trying to hide behind The Galloping Gazelle as the desk melted away—and The Masked Mutant rose up in its place.

His dark eyes burned menacingly through the slits in his mask. He was a lot taller than he appeared in the comic. And a lot more powerful-looking.

And a lot scarier.

He raised a fist at The Galloping Gazelle. "You dare to invade my private office?" he demanded.

"Say goodbye to all this ill-gotten splendour," The Galloping Gazelle told the Mutant.

"I'll say goodbye to *you!*" The Masked Mutant shot back, spitting the words angrily.

Then he turned his frightening, cold eyes on me. "I'll handle you easily, Gazelle," the world's most evil supervillain said softly. "But, *first*, watch me destroy the kid!"

I shrank back as The Masked Mutant took a step towards me, his fist still raised, his black eyes glaring furiously into mine.

My heart pounding, I turned and frantically searched for a hiding place.

But there was nowhere to hide.

And I couldn't make a run for it. The door slammed shut as The Masked Mutant moved closer.

"Whoa!" I cried. I raised both hands in front of my face, as if shielding myself.

I couldn't bear to see his cold, cruel eyes glaring at me as he approached.

He's going to *destroy* me, I thought. But I don't have to watch!

And, then, as The Masked Mutant took one more step, The Galloping Gazelle moved to block his way. "You'll deal with *me*, Mutant!" he declared in his booming voice. "If you want the kid, you'll have to take me out first."

"No problem," The Masked Mutant declared softly.

But his expression changed as The Galloping Gazelle began to circle him. Faster and faster—until the Gazelle appeared to disappear into a whirling, spinning tornado of blue and red.

The Gazelle is carrying out his plan, I realized as I backed up to the wall. He's going to run faster and faster around The Masked Mutant until he creates a whirlwind that will blow the evil Mutant away.

Pressing my back against the wall, I watched the amazing battle eagerly. The Galloping Gazelle whirled faster. Faster. So fast, a powerful wind swept over the room, slapping the curtains, toppling over a vase of flowers, sending books flying from the shelves.

Yes! I thought happily, shooting both fists into the air. *Yes!* We win! We win!

I lowered my hands and let out a horrified groan when I saw The Masked Mutant casually stick his foot out.

The Galloping Gazelle tripped over the foot and slammed face down on to the floor with a shattering *thud*.

He bounced hard a couple of times and then lay still.

The wind stopped. The curtains fell back in place.

The Masked Mutant stood over the fallen

superhero, hands triumphantly on the waist of his costume.

"Get up!" I screamed, without even realizing I was doing it. "Get up, Gazelle! Please!"

The Gazelle groaned, but didn't move.

"Dinnertime," sneered The Masked Mutant.

My back pressed hard against the wall, I stared in horror as The Mutant began to change again. His face twisted and appeared to flatten. His body lowered, and he leaned forward, spreading his hands on the floor.

He stepped forward as a snarling leopard. Tilting its head to one side, the leopard uttered a ferocious growl of attack.

Then it arched its back, tensed its back legs— and leaped on to the sprawled body of The Galloping Gazelle.

"Get up! Get up, Gazelle!" I shrieked as the leopard attacked.

The Masked Mutant clawed and gnawed at the helpless Gazelle.

"Get up! Get *up*!" I screamed.

To my shock, The Galloping Gazelle opened his eyes.

The ferocious leopard ripped away the bottom of The Gazelle's mask with its teeth.

The Galloping Gazelle rolled out from under the enormous beast and scrambled to his feet.

With a roar, the leopard swiped its paws,

sending a long tear down the length of The Gazelle's cape.

"I'm *outta* here!" The Gazelle cried, making tracks to the door. He turned back to me. "You're on your own, kid!"

"No! Wait!" I screamed.

I don't think The Gazelle heard me. He shoved open the door with one shoulder and vanished.

The door slammed behind him.

Quickly, the leopard changed, rising up on its hind legs, its body shifting and moving—until The Masked Mutant stepped forward.

He smiled at me as he approached, a cold, menacing smile.

"You're on your own, kid," he said softly.

I edged along the wall as The Masked Mutant moved slowly, steadily towards me. I knew I couldn't get to the door, as The Galloping Gazelle had. I wasn't fast enough.

He should call himself The Galloping *Chicken*! I thought bitterly.

How could he save his own skin and leave me here like this?

I couldn't run. I couldn't fight. What could I do?

What could I do against a deadly foe who could turn himself into anything solid?

The Masked Mutant stopped in the centre of the room, hands on his waist, his dark eyes twinkling. He was enjoying my fright. And already tasting his victory.

"What are your powers, kid?" he demanded, a sneer in his voice.

"Huh?" His question caught me by surprise.

"What are your powers?" he repeated

impatiently, swirling his cape behind him. "Do you shrink down to a tiny bug? Is that your secret?"

"Huh? Shrink? Me?" I was shaking so hard, I couldn't think straight.

Why was he asking me these questions?

"Do you burst into flames?" he continued, moving closer. "Is that your power? Are you magnetic? Are you a mind-fogger?" His voice turned angry. "What *is* it? *Answer* me! What is your power?"

"I—I don't have any powers," I stammered. If I pressed any harder into the wall, I'd become part of the wallpaper!

The Masked Mutant laughed. "So you won't tell me, huh? Okay, okay. Have it your way."

His smile faded. His dark eyes turned cold and hard. "I was just trying to make it easy on you," he said, moving even closer. "I want to destroy you in the easiest way possible."

"Oh. I see," I muttered.

My eye caught something on the shelf. A large, smooth stone as big as a coconut. It was some kind of decoration. I wondered if it would make a good weapon.

"Say bye-bye, kid," he said through clenched teeth.

He came towards me quickly.

And as he moved, I grabbed the big stone off the shelf. It was a lot heavier than I'd thought. It wasn't stone, I realized. It was shaped like a smooth stone. But it was made of solid steel.

I hoisted it up and took careful aim. Then I heaved it at The Masked Mutant's head.

And missed.

The stone thudded heavily on to the carpet.

"Nice try," he muttered . . .

. . . and moved quickly to destroy me.

I tried to duck away from him, but he was too quick.

His powerful hands grabbed me around the waist and lifted me off the floor.

Higher. Higher.

I realized he was moving his molecules, making his arms stretch until he had lifted me above the chandelier.

I thrashed my arms and legs and tried to squirm away. But he was too strong.

Higher. Higher. Until my head banged hard against the ceiling, at least twenty feet above the floor.

"Happy landings!" The Masked Mutant cried gleefully as he prepared to drop me and send me plummeting to my doom.

But before he could drop me, I heard the door swing open.

The Masked Mutant heard it, too. Holding me suspended in the air, he turned to see who had entered. "You!" he cried in surprise.

High above the floor, I squirmed around and bent my head to see through the chandelier. The light sparkled through the crystals, making it impossible to see.

"How dare you burst in here!" The Masked Mutant cried to the intruder.

He lowered me a little. Just enough for me to see the doorway.

"Libby!" I cried. "What are *you* doing here?"

The Masked Mutant lowered me to the floor and turned to face Libby. My legs were wobbling so badly, I had to grab on to a bookshelf to hold myself up.

"Libby—get *out* of here! Get away!" I tried to warn her.

But she stormed into the room, her red hair flying behind her. She had her eyes on me and completely ignored The Masked Mutant.

Doesn't she *know* that he is the most evil supervillain in the known universe?

"Skipper—didn't you hear me calling you?" Libby demanded sharply.

"Huh? Libby—"

"I was across the street," she said. "I saw you going into this building. I called to you."

"I—I didn't hear you," I stammered. "Listen, you'd better get *out* of here, Libby."

"I've been searching and searching for you," she continued, ignoring my warning, ignoring my frantic gestures. "What are you *doing* in here, Skipper?"

"Uh . . . I really can't talk right now," I replied, pointing to The Masked Mutant.

He stood impatiently, hands at his waist, tapping his boot on the carpet. "I see that I will have to destroy you both," he said quietly.

Libby spun around. She seemed to notice the supervillain for the first time. "Skipper and I are leaving now," she said with a sneer.

I gasped. *Didn't she know who she was talking to?*

No. Of course she didn't know. She reads only *High School Harry & Beanhead* comics. She has no idea how much danger we are in! I realized.

"I'm sorry," The Masked Mutant replied, sneering back at Libby from under his mask. "You are not leaving. In fact, you are never leaving this building again."

Libby glared back at him, and I saw her expression change. Her green eyes grew wide, and her mouth dropped open.

She took a step back until she stood beside me. "We have to do something," she whispered.

Do something?

What could *we* do against the monstrous mega-mutant?

I swallowed hard. I couldn't think of how to answer her.

The Masked Mutant tossed back his cape and

took a step towards us. "Which one of you wants to go first?" he demanded softly.

I turned and saw that Libby had backed up to the bookshelves. She pulled a yellow plastic toy gun from her backpack.

"Libby—what are you *doing*?" I whispered. "That's just a toy!"

"I know," she whispered back. "But this is a comic book—right? It can't be real. So if it's a comic book, we can do *anything*!"

She raised the plastic toy pistol and aimed it at The Masked Mutant.

He let out a cold laugh. "What do you plan to do with that toy?" he asked scornfully.

"It only l-looks like a toy," Libby stammered. "It's a Molecule-Melter. Leave this room—or I'll melt all your molecules!"

The Mutant's smile grew wider. "Nice try," he said, flashing two rows of perfect, white teeth.

He narrowed his eyes at Libby and took another step towards her. "I guess you want to go first. I'll try not to hurt you—too much."

Libby held the toy gun in front of her with both hands. She gritted her teeth, preparing to pull the trigger.

"Put down that toy. It can't help you," The Masked Mutant declared, moving closer.

"I'm not kidding," Libby insisted in a shrill voice. "It isn't a toy. It really *is* a Molecule-Melter."

The Masked Mutant laughed again and took another step closer. Then another step.

Libby aimed the gun at The Mutant's chest. She pulled the trigger.

A high-pitched whistle burst out of the gun.

The Masked Mutant took another step closer. Then another.

Libby lowered the plastic gun.

We both stared in horror as The Masked Mutant came nearer.

He took one more step. Then stopped.

A bright white light circled his body. The light became a crackling electrical current.

The Mutant uttered a low moan. Then he began to melt.

His head melted down into his mask. Tinier and tinier—until it disappeared completely. The empty mask slumped on to the shoulders of his costume. And then the rest of his body melted away, shrinking until there was nothing left but a wrinkled costume and cape, heaped on the carpet.

Libby and I stood staring down at the costume in silence.

"It—it worked!" I finally managed to choke out. "The toy gun—it worked, Libby!"

"Of course," she replied with surprising calm.

She walked over to the empty costume and kicked it with her trainer. "Of course it worked. I warned him it was a Molecule-Melter. He wouldn't listen."

My brain was doing flip-flops. I didn't really understand. It was just a toy pistol. Why did it destroy the mightiest mutant on Earth?

"Let's get out of here!" I pleaded, starting towards the door.

Libby moved to block my path. "I'm sorry, Skipper," she said softly.

"Sorry? What do you mean?"

She raised the plastic pistol and aimed it at me. "I'm sorry," she said, "because you're disappearing next."

At first I thought Libby was joking. "Libby, put down the gun," I told her. "You have a *sick* sense of humour!"

She kept the plastic gun aimed at my chest.

I let out a feeble laugh.

But I quickly cut it short when I saw the hard expression on her face. "Libby—what's your problem?" I demanded.

"I'm not Libby," she replied softly. "I hate to break the news to you, Skipper—but there *is* no Libby."

As she said those words, she began to change. Her red hair slid into her head. Her cheeks grew wider. Her nose lengthened. Her eyes changed from green to black.

She stretched up, growing taller. Muscles bulged on her skinny arms. And as she grew, her clothing changed, too. Her jeans and T-shirt appeared to melt away—replaced by a familiar-looking costume.

The costume of The Masked Mutant.

"Libby—what's going on?" I cried in a tiny, frightened voice. I still didn't understand. "How are you doing that?"

She shook her head. "You don't catch on very fast, do you?" she said, rolling her eyes. Her voice came out deep and booming. A man's voice.

"Libby, I—"

She swept her cape behind her. "I'm The Masked Mutant, Skipper. I changed my molecules into a girl your age and called myself Libby. But I'm The Masked Mutant."

"But—but—but—" I sputtered.

She tossed the toy gun aside and grinned at me triumphantly.

"But you just *melted* The Masked Mutant!" I cried. "We both saw him melt!"

She shook her head. "No. You're mistaken. I just melted The Magnificent Molecule Man."

I gaped at her in astonishment. "Huh? Molecule Man?"

"He worked for me," she explained, glancing down at the crumpled, empty costume on the floor. "Sometimes I ordered him to dress like me. To keep people off my track."

"He worked for you—and you *melted* him?" I cried.

"I'm a villain," The Masked Mutant replied, smiling. "I do very bad things—remember?"

It all started to come clear. There never was a Libby. It had been The Masked Mutant all along.

The Masked Mutant stepped over the crumpled costume to move closer to me. Once again, I pressed my back against the wall. "Now I have no choice. Now I have to do something very bad to you, Skipper," he said flatly, his black eyes staring hard into mine through his mask.

"But—why?" I cried. "Why can't I just leave? I'll go straight home. I'll never tell anyone about you. Really!" I pleaded.

He shook his head. "I can't let you leave. You belong here now."

"Huh?" I gasped. "What are you *saying*, Libby—I mean, Mutant?"

"You belong here now, Skipper," he replied coldly. "I knew it when I saw you on the bus for the first time. I knew you were perfect when you told me you knew *everything* about my comics."

"But—but—" I sputtered again.

"It's so hard to find good characters for my stories, Skipper. It's so hard to find good foes. I'm always looking for new faces. That's why I was so pleased when I discovered you."

His evil grin grew wider. "Then when you recognized my headquarters building, I knew you were right. I knew you were ready to star in a story."

357

The smile faded quickly. "I'm so sorry, Skipper. But the story is over. Your part has come to an end."

"What—what are you going to do?" I stammered.

"Destroy you, of course!" The Mutant replied coldly.

I pressed my back against the wall. I stared back at him, thinking hard.

"Goodbye, Skipper," The Masked Mutant said softly.

"But you can't do this!" I screamed. "You're just a character in a comic book! But I'm real! I'm a real, live person! I'm a real boy!"

A strange smile formed on The Mutant's lips. "No, you're not, Skipper," he said, sniggering. "You're not real. You're just like me now. You're a comic book character, too."

I pinched my arm. It felt as warm and real as always.

"You're a liar!" I shouted.

The Masked Mutant nodded. A pleased smile formed on his face. "Yes, I'm a liar," he agreed. "That's one of my *better* qualities." His smile faded. "But I'm not lying this time, Skipper. You're not real any more."

I refused to believe him. "I feel the way I always have," I declared.

"But I changed you into a comic book character," he insisted. "Remember when you entered this building for the first time? Remember when you walked through the glass door and a beam of light passed over you?"

I nodded. "Yes. I remember that," I muttered.

"Well, that was a scanner," The Masked Mutant continued. "When you stepped through it, it scanned your body. It turned you into tiny dots of ink."

"No!" I shouted.

He ignored my cry. "That's all you are now, Skipper. Tiny dots of red, blue, and yellow ink. You're a comic book character, just like me."

He slid towards me menacingly, his cape spreading out behind him. "But I'm sorry to say you've made your last appearance in my comic book. Or in *any* comic book."

"Wait!" I cried.

"I can't wait any longer," The Masked Mutant replied coldly. "I've already wasted too much time on you, Skipper."

"But I'm not Skipper!" I declared.

"I'm not Skipper Matthews," I said. "There *is* no Skipper Matthews."

"Oh, really?" he asked, rolling his eyes. "Then who are you?"

"I'm The Colossal Elastic Boy!" I replied.

The Masked Mutant uttered a low gasp. "Elastic Boy!" he exclaimed. "I *thought* you looked familiar!"

"Goodbye, Mutant," I said in a deep voice.

"Where are you going?" he asked sharply.

"Back to my home planet of Xargos," I replied, starting towards the door. "I'm not allowed to guest-star in other comic books."

He moved quickly to block the door. "Nice try, Elastic Boy," he said. "But you have invaded my secret headquarters. I have to destroy you."

I laughed. "You can't destroy Elastic Boy!" I boasted. "I'll stretch out my elastic arms and wrap you in them, and squeeze you into Play-Doh!"

"I don't think so," The Masked Mutant replied dryly. He let out an angry growl. "I'm tired of all this talk, talk, talk. I'm going to tear you to pieces—and then tear your pieces into tiny pieces!"

I laughed again. "No way!" I told him. "I'm elastic, remember? I *can't* be torn into pieces. I bend—but I don't break! There's only one way that Elastic Boy can be destroyed!"

"What's that?" The Masked Mutant asked.

"By sulphuric acid," I replied. "That's the only thing that can destroy my elastic body!"

A pleased smile spread behind the masked face.

"Oops!" I cried. "I didn't mean to let that slip out!"

I tried to make it to the door. But I wasn't fast enough.

I saw The Masked Mutant quickly begin to change. He changed into a steaming hot wave of sulphuric acid.

And before I could move, the tall wave of acid swept towards me.

With a loud cry, I leaped away.

The tall wave swept past. It missed me by inches.

I turned and watched it splash over the carpet. The carpet began to sizzle and burn.

"Yes!" I shouted gleefully. "Yes!"

I had never felt so happy, so strong, so triumphant!

I had defeated The Masked Mutant. I had totally tricked him. I had destroyed the most evil supervillain ever to walk the planet!

Me! A twelve-year-old boy named Skipper Matthews! I had sent The Masked Mutant to his doom!

Such a simple trick. But it had worked.

From reading the comics, I knew that The Masked Mutant could change his molecules into anything solid. And then change back again.

But I tricked him into changing himself into a

liquid! And once he changed into a liquid, he could not re-form himself.

The Masked Mutant was gone for ever.

"Skipper, you are a clever guy!" I shouted out loud. I was so happy, I did a little dance on the thick carpet.

I couldn't *believe* The Masked Mutant had believed that I was Elastic Boy. I'd made that name up. I've never *heard* of any Elastic Boy!

But he fell for it. And now the evil supervillain is gone! I thought happily.

And I am alive! Alive!

I couldn't wait to get home and see my family again. The bus ride seemed to take hours.

Finally, I was running up my front lawn. Into the house through the front door.

I immediately saw a brown envelope lying on the mail table. The new issue of *The Masked Mutant*.

Who needs it? I asked myself.

I ignored it and hurried to say hi to my parents. I was so glad to be home, I was even happy to see Mitzi. "Mitzi—how about a game of Frisbee?" I asked.

"Huh?" She gaped at me in shock. I never want to play anything with my little sister.

But, today, I just wanted to be happy and celebrate being alive.

Mitzi and I hurried out to the back garden. We

threw a Frisbee around for about half an hour. We had a great time.

"How about a snack?" I asked her.

"Yeah, I'm starving," she replied. "Mum left some chocolate cake on the counter."

Chocolate cake sounded just right.

Humming happily to myself, I trotted into the kitchen. I pulled down two plates from the cabinet. Then I found the big cake knife in the drawer.

"Don't make your slice bigger than mine!" Mitzi warned, watching me carefully as I prepared to cut the cake.

"Mitzi, I promise I won't cheat you," I said sweetly. I was in such a good mood, even Mitzi couldn't get me upset.

"This looks like awesome chocolate cake!" I exclaimed.

I slid the big knife over the cake.

It slipped.

"Ow!" I cried out as the knife blade cut the back of my hand.

I raised my hand and stared down at the cut. "Hey!" I uttered in surprise.

What was trickling out from the cut?

Not blood.

It was red, blue, yellow, and black.

INK!

"Cool!" Mitzi cried.

"Where's that new *Masked Mutant* comic?" I asked. I suddenly had the feeling that my comic book career wasn't over!

R.L. Stine

Reader beware, you're in for a scare!
These terrifying tales will send shivers up your spine:

1	Welcome to Dead House
2	Say Cheese and Die!
3	Stay Out of the Basement
4	The Curse of the Mummy's Tomb
5	Monster Blood
6	Let's Get Invisible
7	Night of the Living Dummy
8	The Girl Who Cried Monster
9	Welcome to Camp Nightmare
10	The Ghost Next Door
11	The Haunted Mask
12	Piano Lessons Can Be Murder
13	Be Careful What You Wish For
14	The Werewolf of Fever Swamp
15	You Can't Scare Me
16	One Day at HorrorLand
17	Why I'm Afraid of Bees
18	Monster Blood II
19	Deep Trouble
20	Go Eat Worms
21	Return of the Mummy
22	The Scarecrow Walks at Midnight
23	Attack of the Mutant
24	My Hairiest Adventure
25	A Night in Terror Tower

26 The Cuckoo Clock of Doom

27 Monster Blood III

28 Ghost Beach

29 Phantom of the Auditorium

30 It Came From Beneath the Sink!

31 Night of the Living Dummy II

32 The Barking Ghost

33 The Horror at Camp Jellyjam

34 Revenge of the Garden Gnomes

35 A Shocker on Shock Street

36 The Haunted Mask II

37 The Headless Ghost

38 The Abominable Snowman of Pasadena

39 How I Got My Shrunken Head

40 Night of the Living Dummy III

41 Bad Hare Day

42 Egg Monsters From Mars

43 The Beast From the East

44 Say Cheese and Die – Again!

45 Ghost Camp

Goosebumps

Reader beware – here's THREE TIMES the scare!

Look out for these bumper GOOSEBUMPS editions. With three spine-tingling stories by R.L. Stine in each book, get ready for three times the thrill … three times the scare … three times the GOOSEBUMPS!

COLLECTION 1
Welcome to Dead House
Say Cheese and Die
Stay Out of the Basement

COLLECTION 2
The Curse of the Mummy's Tomb
Let's Get Invisible!
Night of the Living Dummy

COLLECTION 3
The Girl Who Cried Monster
Welcome to Camp Nightmare
The Ghost Next Door

COLLECTION 4
The Haunted Mask
Piano Lessons Can Be Murder
Be Careful What You Wish For

COLLECTION 5
The Werewolf of Fever Swamp
You Can't Scare Me!
One Day at HorrorLand

COLLECTION 6
Why I'm Afraid of Bees
Deep Trouble
Go Eat Worms

COLLECTION 7
Return of the Mummy
The Scarecrow Walks at Midnight
Attack of the Mutant

Reader beware – you choose the scare!

Give Yourself Goosebumps

A scary new series from R.L. Stine – where
you decide what happens!

1 Escape From the Carnival of Horrors
2 Tick Tock, You're Dead!
3 Trapped in Bat Wing Hall
4 The Deadly Experiments of Dr Eeek
5 Night in Werewolf Woods

Choose from over 20 scary endings!

HIPPO GHOST

Summer Visitors
Emma thinks she's in for a really boring summer,
until she meets the Carstairs family on the beach.
But there's something very *strange* about her
new friends. . .
Carol Barton

Ghostly Music
Beth loves her piano lessons. So why have they
started to make her *ill*. . .?
Richard Brown

A Patchwork of Ghosts
Who is the evil-looking ghost tormenting Lizzie,
and why does he want to hurt her...?
Angela Bull

The Ghosts who Waited
Everything's changed since Rosy and her family
moved house. Why has everyone suddenly
turned against her. . .?
Dennis Hamley

The Railway Phantoms
Rachel has visions. She dreams of two children
in strange, disintegrating clothes. And it seems
as if they are trying to contact her...
Dennis Hamley

The Haunting of Gull Cottage
Unless Kezzie and James can find what really
happened in Gull Cottage that terrible night
many years ago, the haunting may never stop...
Tessa Krailing

The Hidden Tomb
Can Kate unlock the mystery of the curse on
Middleton Hall, before it destroys the Mason
family...?
Jenny Oldfield

The House at the End of Ferry Road
The house at the end of Ferry Road has just
been built. So it can't be haunted, can it...?
Martin Oliver

Beware! This House is Haunted
This House is Haunted Too!
Jessica doesn't believe in ghosts. So who *is*
writing the strange, spooky messages?
Lance Salway

The Children Next Door
Laura longs to make friends with the children
next door. But they're not quite what they seem. . .
Jean Ure